It was just *her*. He was attracted to her.

And, if he was being honest about this, Josie was being almost annoyingly distant around him. Even though they had just been literally thrown together—and not for the first time—Josie had made absolutely no attempt to move in on him.

She hadn't even flirted with him.

Declan definitely wasn't accustomed to being discounted in this manner. On the contrary, the women who approached him for riding lessons would, at some point or other, make advances on him, attempting to stir him up in some fashion.

He had always taken it as a challenge not to react in any way to any of these women. The reason for that was because he didn't want the lines between his riding student and him to blur.

For the very first time in his life, Declan found that he was willing to allow those lines to get blurry. To his surprise, it was Josie who was the one who seemed determined that they should each stay in their separate lanes and not mix pleasure with business.

Dear Reader,

When I was a kid growing up in New York City, I desperately wanted to have a pet. A cute little dog that would follow me around and do my bidding. But when I asked for a pet, my loving parents could only afford to give me two brothers, who did follow me around but would never do my bidding unless I threatened them with bodily harm. Consequently, I had to wait until I had children of my own before a pet finally became part of our household.

The first one, Rocky (whom my son named because that was his *Rocky* stage—Rocky, by the way, was a female), came from a breeder. Rocky's father was a guard dog imported from Germany. By the age of one, Rocky turned out to behave like a junkyard dog and was extremely fussy when it came to food. She also only liked a very small circle of people she knew. The rest were known to run for the hills.

Our second dog came from the German Shepherd Rescue of Orange County. Once she stopped shaking (she had been abused), she became the most docile, loving dog I've ever had the good fortune to know. She was the embodiment of mellow, and I loved her very much.

Our latest addition is Lucy (also from the rescue society), who loves my husband dearly, on occasion will guard him if I try to come near him and is pure energy in a fur coat. After a year and a half, she still can't be calmly walked (she wants to catch every rabbit who dares to cross her path), but we have high hopes...

As always, I thank you for taking the time to pick up one of my books and from the bottom of my heart, I wish you someone to love who loves you back (and while you're waiting, get a dog).

All the best,

Marie

More Than a Temporary Family

MARIE FERRARELLA

HARLEQUIN
SPECIAL
EDITION

Special thanks and acknowledgment
are given to Marie Ferrarella for her contribution
to the Furever Yours miniseries.

Recycling programs
for this product may
not exist in your area.

ISBN-13: 978-1-335-40848-8

More Than a Temporary Family

For questions and comments about the quality of this book, please contact us at CustomerService@Harlequin.com.

Harlequin Enterprises ULC
22 Adelaide St. West, 41st Floor
Toronto, Ontario M5H 4E3, Canada
www.Harlequin.com

Printed in U.S.A.

USA TODAY bestselling and RITA® Award—winning author **Marie Ferrarella** has written more than three hundred books for Harlequin, some under the name Marie Nicole. Her romances are beloved by fans worldwide. Visit her website, marieferrarella.com.

Books by Marie Ferrarella

Harlequin Special Edition

Forever, Texas

The Cowboy's Lesson in Love
The Lawman's Romance Lesson
Her Right Hand Cowboy
Secrets of Forever

Matchmaking Mamas

Coming Home for Christmas
Dr. Forget-Me-Not
Twice a Hero, Always Her Man
Meant to Be Mine
A Second Chance for the Single Dad
Christmastime Courtship
An Engagement for Two
Adding Up to Family
Bridesmaid for Hire
Coming to a Crossroads
The Late Bloomer's Road to Love

Visit the Author Profile page
at Harlequin.com for more titles.

To
Rocky,
Audrey
And
Lucy
Three German Shepherds
Who Left Their Paw Prints
All Over My
Heart
(Lucy Is Still Leaving Them)

Prologue

Josie Whitaker carefully tiptoed into the nursery, although, she thought wryly, one of the twins was making enough noise to wake the dead while the other, for some mysterious reason, was sound asleep.

However, it wasn't six-month-old Lucas or his sister, Lily, who Josie was thinking about. She was trying not to startle her sister-in-law, Rebekah, who looked as if she was beyond exhausted and on her way to becoming a complete zombie of the old-school variety. The ones who weren't aware of going through the paces of doing things while they were doing them.

The exceedingly frazzled Rebekah was in the small nursery, sitting in the rocking chair Grant, Josie's younger brother, had bought for his wife. The young mother was rocking Lily, trying to get the infant to finally fall asleep before her jarring cries wound up waking her twin brother.

Moving as carefully as a seasoned cat burglar, Josie very slowly placed her hands on Rebekah's shoulders.

The latter did appear to be startled although not with any display of energy. Rebekah looked far too tired for that. Josie had overheard her talking to Grant, saying she viewed her as nothing short of a blessed lifesaver, who, if not endowed with the ability to walk on water, was at least able to restore much needed order in the household, which, right now, was a totally priceless commodity.

"Josie," Rebekah whispered as if the other woman's name said everything there was to be said.

"Why don't you let me take over?" Josie suggested gently.

It wasn't really a question since the older woman was already slipping her very capable hands beneath the baby's bottom, picking Lily up and summarily taking over the baby's care.

"You heard her crying," Rebekah murmured needlessly as she surrendered the tearful tiny burden to her sister-in-law.

"The entire state of North Carolina heard Lily crying," Josie told her with a smile.

Since she had moved from Florida to Spring Forest, North Carolina, and been installed in her brother's garage apartment, she had been doing all she could to help the beleaguered couple juggle everything entailed in being first-time parents. Not only that, but she was helping Rebekah manage her work at an animal rescue shelter as well.

Remembering what it was like when she had been a new mother, Josie had done her best to help the young couple find their footing in this brand-new chaotic world of parenthood that they were trying so hard to navigate.

Josie glanced over her shoulder toward Lucas's crib. Miraculously, the twin still appeared to be sound asleep. She watched the baby's chest to make sure it was moving. It was. He was just, blessedly, a very sound sleeper.

"Lucas seems to be the only one who hasn't heard his sister's cries," his aunt commented with an amused smile.

Rebekah's look of exhaustion melted into one of concern as she regarded her baby. "*Why* doesn't he hear Lily? Why doesn't her crying wake him up? You don't think there's something wrong with his hearing, do you?"

Josie thought of the way the baby had responded to the lullaby she had sung to him last night. He had giggled when she'd made her voice go up extra high. If he could differentiate between sounds, then he could definitely hear.

"No, I don't," Josie answered confidently, continuing to rock Lily. "I think you should just be grateful for the mysterious respite. Now go to bed, 'Mama' before Lucas decides to wake up and join in the 'fun.' Shoo," she added, waving Rebekah off with one hand.

Rebekah's face softened. "I don't know how to thank you."

"You can thank me by going to bed," Josie told her, nodding toward the bedroom door.

Rebekah's feet were already moving in that direction. Whether the young woman was actually conscious of it or not was another story, Josie thought with a smile. Her sister-in-law desperately needed to get some sleep before she wound up collapsing.

"*Go*," Josie mouthed, knowing they were on borrowed time and that Lucas could wake up at any moment.

Josie sighed softly as her sister-in-law left the room.

"Alone at last," she murmured to the bundle in her arms. For her part, Lily was finally settling down. She was awfully cute when she wasn't screaming her lungs out.

Rebekah and Grant were still thanking her almost daily for uprooting her life and coming to stay with them. But quite honestly, she was as grateful to them as they were to her. She enjoyed looking after the babies. And helping them out gave her a purpose.

After a life that had been nothing but nonstop work as she'd focused on putting her husband through medical school—even after their daughter, Hannah, had been born—her whirlwind existence had come to an almost abrupt, screeching halt in the last four years. Her less than grateful husband had opened up his practice and the rest of it had turned into a cliché when he'd had an affair with his nurse.

Ultimately, he'd chosen his nurse over Josie, turning his back on both her and their daughter, leaving them behind.

For some reason, perhaps to win over her father, Hannah had decided to become a doctor just like him and, after high school graduation, had gone off to a premed college program in another state. She'd then elected to double up on courses so she could expedite getting her degree.

While she was supportive of her daughter's choices, that had suddenly left Josie's once extremely busy life extremely empty.

Oh sure, back in Florida she'd had her catering business, but now that she was in Spring Forest that did little to fill her life. More than anything, Josie liked being needed. So when she'd learned about her brother and sister-in-law's situation, she was more than eager to volunteer to help them out. Josie had firsthand knowledge what it was like, trying to raise a baby while holding down a job.

In a way, she felt like this was déjà vu—except that she got to hold the babies in her arms instead of leaving that up to friends who were able to pitch in.

In another way, she thought, she was now living that part of her life she had sorely missed out on. Even though she had never complained to her husband during those years, she would have much rather just been a stay-at-home mom and raised Hannah rather than working to pay the bills.

"You're my second chance," she whispered to Lily.

Lily responded by finally falling asleep.

Josie went on rocking to ensure that the twin was really asleep. Besides, it felt wonderful holding a baby in her arms.

She went on rocking a long time.

Chapter One

Declan Hoyt had never entertained any delusions of grandeur. He had never wanted to be famous or even have an inordinate amount of money in his bank account. All he'd ever wanted was to be a successful horse breeder. It had been a dream of his as far back as he could remember. In his heart, he didn't think he'd been asking for that much.

But, he had learned, the funny thing about plans was that no matter how simple they seemed to be on the outset, they had a way of either getting complicated or going sideways.

His certainly had.

It wasn't all that long after he began pursuing his career that Declan discovered being a small-time horse breeder didn't begin to bring in enough money to pay the bills. So he'd begun to board horses for other people. When that still hadn't brought in enough money, he'd branched out and started giving riding lessons as well.

Normally a very frugal man, Declan had found himself in need of even more extra money after his father died unexpectedly a year ago and his mother, Ruth, just fell to pieces over the loss. Distraught, it had taken his mother practically the whole year to pull herself together.

Not about to abandon his mother, Declan had come to her rescue by taking her in to live with him.

That simple act had helped Ruth come around. Slowly but surely, she'd found that she was able to cope with the unending sea of loneliness that had threatened to completely engulf her in the beginning. Wanting to show her gratitude—as well as remain useful—Ruth had taken over the cooking as well as the maintenance of the farmhouse for Declan.

It had taken almost a year, but things were beginning to look as if they were finally settling down for Declan and his mother.

But fate had a way of throwing the proverbial monkey wrench into the works—or at least it felt that way to Declan. In his particular case, the monkey wrench came in the form of his younger sister Peggy. Even at her best, Peggy had never been very emotionally stable and, as luck would have it, his sister hadn't married the model of stability either. The problems had come for both of them when Peggy'd started self-medicating her depression and anxiety with a variety of substances that had only made things worse. Two years and one baby girl later, Peggy's husband had decided that he'd had enough of his wife's drinking as well as her doing drugs, so he'd taken off.

Unfortunately, it seemed that the stress brought upon by her husband's abandonment had only made Peggy's issues that much more pronounced. Despite her family's offers to help, her answer had been to soothe her pain with more alcohol and harder drugs.

Periodically, Peggy would declare her desire to be a better mother to her little one. To that end, she would dutifully check herself into some rehab center or other. During those times—and there were more than a few—Peggy would leave her daughter, Shannon, in her parents' care.

That was all well and good when there'd been two of them to share the burden of watching over and taking care of Shannon. But after Ruth's husband died, Ruth had found she didn't have the wherewithal to put up with a now fourteen-year-old distressed teenager.

Besides, Ruth no longer had a home where the girl could go. She was now living in Declan's house, which meant that Shannon had to go there.

And just like that, Declan found his once very simple life become extremely complicated. Between caring for his mother and his teenaged niece as well as all the extra jobs he took on the side, the six-foot-two, thirty-eight-year-old horse breeder/farmer had his hands more than full.

To say the least, he did not take the news of this latest invasion of his home front very well.

"There's nobody else she can stay with?" Declan wanted to know when his mother had dropped this latest bombshell into his life. That was when he discovered that, in trouble again, his sister'd had a choice of going into a ninety-day rehab program or serving actual jail time.

Peggy had naturally chosen the rehab program, which meant that Shannon had to come stay with her grandmother—and that meant with him.

"You know there isn't," Ruth told her son in an apologetic tone. "Shannon either stays here with you—with us," his mother amended, "or Children's Services will take her to live at one of their facilities. You don't want that, do you?" Ruth asked, looking at her son for confirmation. The idea of something like that happening to her granddaughter was clearly unbearable.

"No," Declan reluctantly agreed with a sigh, knowing his mother wouldn't give up pressing him until she heard the answer she wanted to hear, "we don't." For now, he kept his concern that he wouldn't be able to support his niece financially or emotionally to himself. His mother didn't need any more on her shoulders. Somehow, he'd find a way to deal with it.

A couple of days later, Declan began to feel that maybe he had given his mother the wrong answer. He found that the fourteen-year-old was less than exactly a ray of sunshine when he had to put up with the teenager on a regular, full-time basis.

"What's wrong with your internet reception?" Shannon wanted to know when he walked into the living room that morning. Her fingers were all but pounding out her irritation on her less than receptive cell phone. She had had her face buried in the electronic device since she'd arrived.

"Good morning to you too," Declan replied sardonically. Then, seeing that his displeasure had completely gone over his niece's head, he said, "The *internet* seems to have a mind of its own," he told her, giving her an annoyed look. "You should know what that's like." Truth be told, Declan wasn't very proficient with the internet himself, and paid someone in town to maintain only the most basic website for his business because he had to. He was doing his best to learn how, because, at bottom, he believed in being a hands-on person.

Shannon's brows drew together as she scowled at him. "A mind of its own," she echoed. "Does that mean I don't have to do those dumb chores you gave me?" the teenager wanted to know, referring to the list her uncle had given her last night.

"No, it does not," he informed her evenly. He found that she made him lose his temper even faster than Peggy had when she was that age—but, as with Peggy, he knew that she was taunting him deliberately to get a reaction. He refused to rise to the bait— or back down. Declan had given his niece a week to settle in, but enough was enough. As far as he was concerned, the vacation was over. Besides, she got moodier every day she sat around with nothing to do. She needed to get out of her head, get some fresh air, and spend a few minutes being productive. It would be good for her, whether she'd admit it or not. "Everyone has to pull their own weight around here."

"Maybe I don't want to pull my own weight," Shannon told him, tossing her head defiantly and sending her red hair flying over her shoulder.

"You like to eat, don't you?" Declan pointedly asked.

"Yes," Shannon replied, drawing the word out as if she thought it was a trick question.

"Then you'll do the chores," he informed her flatly. "It's as simple as that. And I want them done by the time I get back home."

Shannon looked as if she was ready to challenge her uncle's order. "But—"

"The terms are nonnegotiable," Declan informed his niece crisply, shutting her down. And then he turned toward his mother. "See you later, Mom," he told the frail older woman just before he brushed his lips against her cheek.

"Go easy on her, dear," his mother whispered into his ear.

But he had no intentions of doing that. "That's the problem, Mom," he whispered back. Out of the corner of his eye, he could see Shannon leaning in their direction, trying to hear what they were saying.

"Peggy let her do anything she wanted to because my sister was too busy drowning her own sorrows. Well, that's over now. Shannon needs to grow up to be a responsible person, and I want to help her get there. It's up to us to show her that she can do more with her life than follow her mother's example."

"Yes," Ruth agreed hesitantly. "But not all in one day, dear."

But Declan disagreed. "It's got to start sometime, Mom," he informed his mother.

Grabbing his customary baseball cap from the coatrack by the door, he pulled it on and left the house.

Declan definitely was not happy about having someone else to be responsible for when he already had so much on his plate, he thought as he made his way toward his ten-year-old Jeep, but he intended to do his best by the girl, which included making her follow a few rules for her own good.

In his opinion, his parents should have done that with Peggy. But they hadn't.

Well, it might be too late to get his sister out of her destructive cycle, but he wouldn't let Shannon fall into one, too. Shannon might not think of him in glowing terms, but eventually she would come to realize that he had only the best of intentions when it came to her upbringing and her welfare.

Right now, Declan thought as he drove his Jeep toward the area where he stabled the horses he boarded, he had another tenderfoot coming in for a riding lesson. Probably so she could live out her fantasy of being Annie Oakley.

Oh well, the horse breeder shrugged philosophically, he did need the money, so there was no point in even thinking about being picky. The best he could hope for was that the woman wouldn't wind up talking his ear off.

When the call had come in making the appointment for the lessons, he hadn't recognized the voice on the phone or the student's name. It had turned out to be some woman who'd wanted to give her sister-in-law the lessons as a thank-you gift.

In other words, he thought, he was being saddled with a novice.

But then, he wasn't looking to make a lifelong friend, Declan thought. He just wanted someone who wouldn't put too many demands on him.

At least, he considered, he could hope for that.

Getting out of his Jeep, Declan glanced at his watch. He had a little over an hour to spare before he had to move on to the next chore on his list.

Going into the stable, he took a moment then selected a horse for the woman. Marigold was a gentle mare who could have almost doubled for a rocking horse, he mused as he quickly saddled the mare.

Finished, he went on to saddle his own horse, a dignified-looking black stallion named Midnight he had helped to deliver four years ago. Declan was extremely proud of the animal, having gone on to train the horse himself. He was willing to bet there wasn't a finer piece of horseflesh anywhere, but then, he thought with a rare smile, he was hardly unbiased.

"C'mon, boy, we've got a tenderfoot to put up with," he said to the stallion.

Midnight pawed the ground, as if indicating that he understood. At least, that was the way that Declan chose to interpret the movement. Except for his mother, the horse breeder felt that he had more in common with horses than with people. They were certainly easier to understand.

Declan led the two horses out into the adjacent corral, hoping that this "student" knew enough to show up on time and that she'd actually listen to him rather than bend his ear with endless chatter. He had no interest in learning the woman's life story. Not when he was already dealing with too much noise and conversation.

His mother loved to talk—and she needed an audience. His father had had a gift for tuning out what he didn't want to hear, Declan thought with a smile.

Too bad he hadn't passed that talent on to him, the breeder mused. There were times he would have sorely appreciated that talent.

And now, of course, there was Shannon, too. Another voice to add to the echo chamber that existed in his head. It made him long for the days when he got hours of silence as he rode overseeing his horses.

Maybe someday he could do that again, Declan reflected wistfully as he led the two horses behind him.

The breeder stopped abruptly, surprised to see a

woman he didn't recognize standing at the perimeter of the corral. As their eyes met, she looked slightly uneasy. He noticed that hers were a vivid shade of sky blue.

For a moment, he came very close to losing himself in them.

From his experience in giving lessons to other first-time, adult riders, he had just assumed she would be a matronly, slightly out-of-shape woman wearing fancy designer jeans and maybe a shirt that was one size too tight on her.

Instead, his new pupil's outfit looked casual and comfortable. She wasn't out to impress, which he viewed as a plus for her side. The woman had long blond hair that she had put up in a careless, messy bun with strands coming out all over the place.

No, she definitely wasn't looking to impress, he thought.

It took him a moment to suppress the curve that threatened to overtake his lips. The last thing he wanted to deal with was a prima donna who was there hoping to garner covert appreciative looks and trying to make an impression on him.

He had no time for women like that. Or vain people in general, he thought. He had too much on his plate to put up with that.

But the woman *was* rather attractive, he decided. Not that that meant anything one way or another, Declan thought.

"Are you Declan Hoyt?" Josie asked when the tall, broad-shouldered and exceedingly muscular-looking man continued to say nothing even as he regarded her.

"Yeah," Declan finally answered, his monotone indicating that there was nothing more forthcoming.

Maybe her "talkative" instructor was waiting for her name, Josie reasoned.

"I'm Josie Whitaker. I think my sister-in-law called you about giving me a few riding lessons," she said.

"She did," Declan replied.

"It was an early birthday gift," she told him. "From her and my brother," Josie added.

"Uh-huh."

Well, he certainly couldn't be accused of talking her ear off, Josie thought.

"Well, I'm here," she told him in as cheerful a voice as she could muster. She felt as if the cowboy was trying to decide whether or not he *wanted* to give her these lessons. There was no other way for her to interpret his behavior.

"I can see that," Declan answered.

The silence felt almost deafening. Desperate to fill the air with something other than the sound of her charismatic riding teacher's breathing, Josie turned her attention to the black stallion he was holding.

"Aren't you a beauty?" she said, reaching out to pet the stallion's muzzle.

"Midnight's my horse," Declan told her, pulling the stallion back.

Startled, it took her a moment to gather herself. "I wasn't trying to take him," she told her less than warm and fuzzy riding instructor. "I just wanted to pet him," she explained. Her eyes shifted toward the stallion. "You wouldn't mind my petting you, would you, boy?" she asked, slowly holding her hand up to the horse, wrist side up so that he could sniff her and see for himself that she posed no threat.

Declan was about to chastise her to get back, but he never got the chance. He was surprised to observe that his one-man-only stallion seemed to be intrigued by this woman who, from what he had been told, knew absolutely nothing about horses.

Midnight stood regarding this new student as if he wasn't sure what to make of her.

That probably makes two of us, boy, Declan silently told his horse.

"Marigold, here, is your ride," he told Josie, nodding at the mare as he held out her reins.

"Hi, Marigold," Josie said, smiling warmly at the mare. "Pleased to meet you."

She was an odd one, Declan thought. But at least she didn't come across as bossy or privileged. He supposed he should take what he could get.

"Ever been on a horse?" he asked her, although he felt he knew the answer to that.

"Does a merry-go-round horse count?" she asked with a genial smile.

Who the hell would count a wooden horse as a substitute for the real thing? "No," he told her in no uncertain terms.

"Then no," she answered with a wide, engaging grin. "I haven't."

"Terrific," he muttered, his expression indicating that it was anything but that.

This, Josie decided, was going to be a long, silent riding lesson. A *very* long, silent lesson.

Chapter Two

The silence felt as if it was stretching out forever between them.

"So I take it that means you've never ridden a horse before," Declan finally said.

He was looking at her as if she came from another planet, Josie thought.

"There's not much call for horses where I come from in Florida," she told him, doing her best to sound friendly. "But it's always been on my to-do list and I'm eager to learn," she added, hoping that would win this brawny sphinx over.

"Florida," Declan repeated. "Is that where you're from?"

She was surprised that he was showing some interest in her life. She had to admit that it made her a little uneasy. "If I say yes, will you hold that against me too?"

Declan frowned. He hadn't meant to come across as if he was interested in her, although he had to admit that in a way, he was. "I'm not holding anything against you," he told her.

Josie flashed a bright smile at the instructor. "Oh, good to know. My mistake," she willingly acknowledged cheerfully.

He stood there for a moment, not knowing what to make of this woman. And then his eyes narrowed. "You're one of those people who tries to make the best of everything, aren't you?"

She was not about to deny it. After all, it wasn't something she was ashamed of. It had actually helped her get over some very bleak times.

"I try," Josie answered honestly.

Declan decided that his best way out of this discussion was just to focus on the reason why she was there in the first place.

"All right, we'll start with the basics," he told her, his voice devoid of any and all humor. "This is your horse." He held out the reins toward her.

Josie nodded, taking the reins into her hand. She petted the mare's muzzle. "Marigold." She said the name warmly.

"You were listening." There was just a trace of surprise in his voice, as if he really hadn't expected her to have been paying any attention.

"I *always* listen," she told him. There was neither

annoyance nor pride in her voice. She was merely stating a simple fact.

"Admirable quality." He said the words as if he felt he was obligated to.

He was baiting her, Josie thought, and she had no idea why. Maybe he had come here to begin her riding lesson fresh from having an argument with his wife. Whatever the reason, she decided to ignore it.

Instead, she answered, "I find paying attention saves a lot of time and keeps me from asking annoying questions I would have known the answer to if I had been listening the first time around."

Somehow, Declan reasoned, that was aimed at him—and he supposed that, in a way, he did deserve it.

He suppressed a sigh. Doing his best to remain neutral, he said, "Okay, let's get started."

"I'd love to," Josie answered with unmistakable enthusiasm. He could have even sworn that her eyes were sparkling.

"Since you've obviously made friends with your mount…" he went on—for some reason, the mare seemed to be responding to this woman faster than he could remember ever observing any of the horses responding to one of his students before. "We will skip the step where you attempt to familiarize yourself with your horse in order to get the horse used to you."

His new student nodded in a manner that made Declan feel as if she were absorbing every single syllable coming out of his mouth. Nobody was that attentive, he thought, but he let it go.

"And what's the next step?" Josie wanted to know.

That was almost too simple to verbalize. But he saw that he had to. "Mounting your horse," he told her.

That sounded easy enough, Josie thought. After all, she had grown up watching classic Westerns on TV thanks to a beloved grandfather who'd doted on the genre. During that time, she must have seen literally dozens of cowboys get on their horses from as many angles. It was all part of the action—she just hadn't paid that much attention to the exact procedure, she realized.

Well, there was a fifty-fifty chance of getting this right, Josie told herself. After all, the mare had two sides.

She picked one.

As she approached her horse, ready to comply with Declan's order, she saw her instructor shaking his head. Josie froze in her tracks.

"Wrong side?" she guessed.

Declan raised an eyebrow. "What do you think?"

It *was* the wrong side, but the bigger problem was that she needed to understand all the steps before just jumping in. He was waiting for her to realize that for herself. People tended to assume that they knew how to ride just because they'd seen others do it before. She had to understand that there was a process she'd need to learn, step by step. Thankfully, she seemed to figure it out before he had to intervene.

Josie blew out a breath. "I think you should show me by getting on your horse first so I can mimic what you do."

Well, at least she was actually willing to learn and didn't have a chip on her shoulder like his last student had—or his niece, for that matter, he added as a postscript.

So far, this wasn't as bad as he had anticipated, Declan thought.

"I've got another idea," he told her.

"You're not going to quit already, are you?" she asked, anticipating the worse outcome. The man's manner made that a very real possibility from where she was standing.

Her question caught Declan off guard. "I never quit," he informed her. He watched the expression that washed over her face. She actually looked visibly relieved. Maybe this really was important to her.

"My idea," he told her, "comes in the form of another suggestion. How about I talk you through this?"

Josie brightened at his proposal. "Okay."

There was that unbridled eagerness again, Declan noted, doing his best not to get caught up in the thoughts that were suddenly materializing in his head. He wasn't there to admire the woman and was certainly not there to be attracted to her. He was there to teach her the basics of horseback riding and send her on her way—and ultimately away from him.

"Get on the other side of the horse," he said,

moving his hand around in a semicircle in case she missed his point.

Josie obediently did as he told her and moved over to the correct side of the animal, then stopped, waiting for further instructions.

"Now insert your left foot into the stirrup, hold on to the saddle, and pull your weight up, then swing your right leg over to follow through," he told her in a singsong voice.

She did exactly what he said, remaining completely calm—at least until she attempted to swing her right leg over the horse's rump. To her surprise, she couldn't.

Her second attempt didn't have any better result than her first attempt. On her third attempt, she felt a hand push against her butt. There was nothing sexual about the contact. It was pragmatic, meant to get her up and over, which it did.

Embarrassed by her need for the boost, Josie glanced at him from her perch. "I never had time for any real exercise regimen."

He had no idea what that had to do with anything, but her statement felt as if it begged for some sort of follow-up from him so, after a moment, he asked, "Why not?"

Without realizing he was doing it, he glanced at his new student's body. He saw nothing out of shape about the woman.

"I was too busy working and putting my husband through medical school to take any time to minister to my own needs," she said in answer to his question.

"Whatever time I had left over after work, I spent with my little girl—when she was a little girl," Josie amended, thinking of the young woman she had sent off to college three years ago.

Without actually asking her for any specific details, he now had two pieces of information that he didn't want. He knew that his student was married and that she had a daughter.

The way she was looking at him, Declan supposed that this now required some sort of response or acknowledgment on his part.

He said the obvious. "So, you're married to a doctor."

Josie surprised him by saying, "No."

Was she playing some sort of a joke on him? "I thought you said you put your husband through medical school. What happened, he flunk out?" Declan asked. Her husband had probably been a kid born to privilege who didn't know how to buckle down and make something of himself. So, while his wife worked, he probably just liked to party. He caught himself feeling somewhat sorry for the woman.

"Only when it came to being a husband," Josie answered honestly as she tried to get comfortable in the saddle. This struck her as being more difficult than she had imagined.

"What happened?" Declan heard himself asking.

She had signed on for forever. Sadly, her ex hadn't.

"Classic story," she said dismissively. "He opened a practice, got a nurse, then left with his nurse to set up a practice, and a marriage, somewhere else."

Declan hadn't expected to get such an honest answer. "Oh. Sorry, I didn't mean to ask such personal questions." He really hadn't, he thought. How did this woman even manage to get him to think along these lines? It wasn't like him. "Let's get back to your lesson," he told her gruffly.

She nodded then said, "That's okay."

She had managed to lose him with that simple phrase. "What's okay?" He was mystified.

Her forgiving smile seemed to penetrate right into his chest. "I don't mind you asking questions."

Her tone sounded almost charitable and that only managed to further rub him the wrong way.

"You're the one who's supposed to be asking questions," he pointed out. "About the horseback riding lesson," he clarified in case there was any doubt in her mind what he was referring to.

Rather than become defensive, which he had to admit he was expecting and braced for, the woman just nodded her head as if accepting his words as gospel.

"Sorry," she apologized again. "I guess I just got caught up in things."

"Stop doing that." He caught himself before he wound up snapping the words at her.

She cocked her head, as if that would help her understand his meaning. It didn't. "Stop doing what?"

"Stop cleaning the slate and giving me a pass as if you were the one who had committed the offense instead of me," he told her in a less than charitable voice. He realized that she wasn't doing this on purpose, but it still irritated him.

Josie shook her head. In her mind, Declan hadn't committed any sort of offense against her. "But you didn't—"

She was doing it again, he thought. Removing all blame from him. He hadn't felt guilty, but now that she was absolving him of it, it seemed to manage to stoke those embers.

"Let's just get on with the lesson," he told her gruffly.

That was the whole reason why she was there and she didn't want to needlessly waste his time. She knew he had to be busy taking care of things. The ranch didn't run itself and, so far, she hadn't seen anyone else, like a hired hand, around.

"Absolutely," she cheerfully agreed.

Declan couldn't help wondering how someone so agreeable could be so annoying at the same time. He took a breath, reminding himself that the woman *was* saying all the right things. There was no reason for him to get his back up like this.

So why was he?

He had no answer for that.

The lesson. Focus on the damn lesson, he told himself. *The sooner you get that out of the way, the sooner you can get back to your other work.*

"Do you know how to make your mount go to the right?" he asked, pulling the question out of the air in a desperate attempt to get the lesson back on track.

Rather than risk making a wrong guess this time, she said, "Tell me."

The woman was a blank slate, Declan thought. She was just waiting for him to write words on it.

She had to be the most agreeable woman he had ever encountered and, right now, he wasn't in the mood for agreeable. Not when his mood was so sour from his confrontation with his niece.

Startled, Declan suddenly realized that he had just admitted, albeit silently, that he was in a bad mood. He supposed, he grudgingly thought, that was a step in the right direction to resolving this internal problem he was having.

He spent the next couple of hours walking Midnight around the corral while giving Josie instructions on the correct way to hold and use the reins to guide her mount, correcting her posture in the saddle, and her feet in the stirrups. He even let her walk the horse as he watched carefully.

"Do you want to go for a ride?" he asked her without any warning.

Josie looked at the horse breeder in surprise. She was doing her best not to make any sudden moves that might cause her to slip off the horse. She still didn't feel all that secure on the mare's back.

"Do you think I'm ready?" she asked the unsmiling cowboy.

"Well, I know you're nervous, but I've been watching you and you're doing better than you realize. Trust me."

If she didn't know any better, she would have said

that his voice had sounded almost light as he'd offered her that last observation.

"I guess so," she answered after a very long beat. Her voice was less than filled with confidence.

"All right," he told her.

Glancing around, Declan found what he was looking for. A goal for her to ride toward. "We'll just take a short ride over to that tree," he told her, pointing it out for Josie's benefit. "Is that all right with you?" he asked as an afterthought.

She was surprised he had even asked. It didn't seem like something he would think of doing. "Why wouldn't it be?"

"Just checking," he told her.

Most of his students were opinionated or difficult to deal with or just interested in flirting with their riding instructor, namely him. His experiences with teaching horseback riding were still rather limited at this point, but he hadn't really run into anyone who was so genuinely interested in wanting to learn the fundamentals from him and nothing more. There was always something else involved in the scenario.

Declan glanced at his student. She had a nice profile, he decided. But the woman definitely didn't seem to have any interest in charming him or exercising her feminine wiles to make herself feel better because her husband was ignoring her.

Oh, that was right, she didn't have a husband—not anymore. The man, he decided, had been a jerk, leaving an attractive woman who had worked hard to put him through medical school. That had been a hell of a thank-you for her efforts and sacrifice, he couldn't help thinking.

"Ready?" he asked, nodding toward the goal he had selected.

"Ready," she answered almost eagerly, her eyes trained on the target.

"Then let's go!" he ordered.

Without meaning to, he sped up his horse, hitting his heels against the stallion's sides. It was just an automatic reaction on his part. He hadn't taken into account that his student wasn't accustomed to riding fast—or at all.

Turning to her, he saw her mimicking his movements almost as if she were a mirror.

And just like that, they were riding toward the tree he had pointed out.

The woman had potential, he caught himself thinking. He continued to rein in his horse so she wasn't tempted to speed up her own mount. He knew how tempting it could be to stay abreast of his horse. He wondered if she knew how easily he could have given Midnight his head and gotten to the tree way ahead of the woman. But no, better to have taken it comparatively slowly.

Because, glancing toward her now, he could see that she was barely hanging on.

Chapter Three

When she finally reached the tree that Declan had pointed out as their designated target, Josie's face was flushed and she was breathing hard. It was almost as if she had been the one running toward the target instead of the mare she was on.

In addition, Josie was grinning from ear to ear like a kid who had managed to win a race no one had expected her to win.

None of this was lost on Declan, especially not the triumphant grin on her face.

Ordinarily, he wouldn't have said anything. But for some reason, it just didn't seem right to maintain his silence. Besides, he had to admit that his new student had thrown herself into this endeavor and had tried harder than any of the other people he had ever taught.

Taking a breath as if to fortify himself, Declan grudgingly said, "Not bad."

Getting a positive comment from Declan was like pulling teeth, she thought, but that didn't diminish the pleased feeling spreading throughout her like an unleashed outpouring of sunshine.

She had a sense that, in Declan's world, what he had just said amounted to very high praise, so she took it as such.

"Thank you," she said as if he had just bestowed a championship medal on her. And then she went on to admit, "I'm just happy I didn't fall off Marigold."

"That makes two of us," Declan murmured, thinking he had uttered the sentiment under his breath.

But Josie obviously heard him. "Don't worry," she told him, "if that had happened, I would have just picked myself up."

He gave her a look then glanced at the distance between her and the ground. It wasn't difficult to tell what he was thinking.

"I would have," Josie insisted.

Something like a wry smile curved his mouth. "Good thing we didn't have to put that to the test," Declan told her then nodded over his shoulder toward the stable. "Ready to go back?"

"Oh, is the lesson over already?" she asked, making no effort to hide the fact that the thought left her somewhat sad. She would have been happy to continue riding, even with a stone-faced teacher.

"No," he answered, surprising her. "I've got one more thing to teach you when we get back to the stable."

Josie became instantly suspicious. "What?" she asked. Declan looked far too pleased with what he was about to say. She braced herself.

"How to unsaddle your mount and put everything away," he told her simply. "No proper rider puts their mount away without removing the saddle and brushing the horse's hide."

To his surprise, she didn't balk or say something to the effect that she thought that was part of his job, the way a few of his other students had when he had told them they needed to unsaddle and groom their horse.

Instead, Josie merely nodded, saying, "I get it. That's a little like giving a baby a bath at the end of the day before putting him or her to bed."

The woman was being an awfully good sport about the fact that he was actually giving her a chore to do, Declan thought. Now that he'd rolled the matter over in his head, he supposed she had also cited a good comparison.

"Yeah, like that," he agreed after a beat. "Are you up for it?" he wanted to know. Part of him was still waiting for her to beg off or come up with some sort of an excuse not to do the chore.

But to his surprise, she didn't.

"Sure," Josie answered cheerfully. "This is all just part of the first lesson, right?" As far as she was concerned, it was a rhetorical question. "I mean the horses don't just come out of the stable, fully saddled and ready to go whenever they're needed, right?"

It took him a second before he realized that she was serious and was waiting for him to agree with her assessment. So he did.

"Right," Declan finally echoed.

Turning his stallion around, he glanced to see if his student had followed suit.

It took Josie a little longer to get her own horse positioned and pointed in the proper direction. Marigold was docile, but not above trying to exercise her own will at times.

"Okay, I'm ready," she announced, pleased that she had managed to get Marigold to face in the same direction as Midnight.

Declan nodded, his expression giving no indication of what he was thinking or the fact that, so far, this new student had actually managed to please him by taking orders without raising any sort of objections or launching into any arguments, irrational or otherwise.

Slanting a glance in her direction to see if the woman was ready, Declan nudged his heels against his stallion's sides, a silent signal for the horse to take off.

Midnight did.

As did, a second later, Josie and Marigold.

The ride back seemed to go quicker than the initial ride to the tree he had picked out. Josie said as much to him once they had reached the stable.

"The way back always seems to be faster," he commented. "That's just the way things turn out."

Josie had her own theory about that. "Probably because the terrain back seems to be a little more familiar than it was on the initial trip out."

"Yeah, probably," he agreed with a grunt.

Declan dismounted in one fluid motion and came to hold Marigold's reins so Josie could do the same. But when Josie attempted to follow his example, it wasn't nearly as fluid. And when her feet met the ground, she was surprised to find that her knees unexpectedly buckled.

She would have fallen straight to the ground if Declan hadn't reacted with lightning speed and just managed to catch her before that happened.

He closed his arms around her and automatically pulled his student up against him. In less than a second's time, there wasn't so much as even an inch of space left between them.

It was hard to say which of them was more startled by the sudden action.

However, Josie was the one who recovered first, flashing a grateful smile at her instructor.

"Thank you. That could have been very awkward," she admitted.

"Could have been?" he questioned.

He would have thought that being pulled up against him like this would have been deemed to be *very* awkward by her.

It certainly would have been for him if he had been in her place, Declan thought.

Josie tried hard to appear as if the act of being pulled up close and personal against her very rugged instructor's chest hadn't sent warm, appreciative ripples undulating all through her.

She honestly couldn't remember the last time she had been this close to a man. It had probably been some time before her marriage had begun to go sour, and that was more than six years ago.

Way more than six years ago, as she recalled.

"Yes. It would have been pretty embarrassing if I had wound up doing a pratfall right at your feet," she freely admitted.

"I'd hardly call what had almost happened just now a pratfall," Declan told her. He wasn't just trying to give her a cover to cling to or help her save face. In his mind, he was just being accurate.

However, his new student saw his comment in a different light. "That's because you're just being kind," she told him.

"I have hardly *ever* been accused of that," he freely told her.

"Maybe not out loud to your face," she allowed.

For a second, Declan thought that was the end of it. But then Josie went on to qualify her answer.

"I mean people would be afraid to say that to you out loud. After all, you do have a rather intimidating manner about you."

That made him feel bad somehow. He wasn't trying to intimidate her, he was just trying to get this lesson over with as quickly as possible because he had things to do. Now that he thought about it, he hadn't really been fair to this woman who had been nothing but amiable and had bent over backward in her attempt to follow his instructions and be accommodating.

And now that he thought about it again, she really had behaved completely differently than anyone he had ever had to deal with.

"Look, you don't have to unsaddle your horse this time," he told her. "I'll take care of it."

"But it's part of the lesson," Josie protested, "and I don't intend to let things slide. I came to get riding lessons so that I could learn everything that was involved, down to the smallest detail, and I fully intend to pull my own weight," she told him. "You just need to talk me through it the first time," she went on. Trying to get him to understand, she told him, "You'll find that when it comes to chores, I'm a very fast learner."

He was surprised that she would say something like that. It wasn't exactly something that most women he knew would admit to, he thought. At least, not when it actually came to chores.

He recalled his last discussion when it came to chores.

"Too bad my niece isn't like you." The words were out of his mouth before Declan was aware of giving voice to them. That had been much too personal an admission, he thought.

"You have a niece?" Josie asked, immediately interested.

"Yes—" he bit off in a less than amicable tone "—I have a niece."

Josie picked up on his tone. "You don't exactly sound all that happy about it."

"That's because she's a royal pain," he answered, surprised at how easily he had admitted that to a woman he barely knew.

There was something about this woman that seemed to just draw the words right out of his mouth, Declan admitted grudgingly. But at least he'd kept back the more personal details—like how much it frustrated him that he didn't know how to make things better, that he was clueless when it came to how to get through to Shannon and keep her from following her mother's path.

Rather than comment on his choice of words, Josie had a question for him. "How old is your niece?" she wanted to know.

Declan saw no reason to withhold this relatively harmless piece of information from the woman.

"She's fourteen," he told her.

"Ah," Josie answered, nodding her head knowingly at the input.

"'Ah'?" he questioned, echoing the word she had used. Just what was that supposed to mean?

She nodded. "Unless she's radically different from other girls her age, this particular age period is what's known as 'the terrible teens.' You'll find yourself being tested at every turn."

"Sounds great," he muttered darkly.

"Hang in there," Josie encouraged. "It does get

better eventually. Your niece is just trying to learn and test her boundaries and limits by seeing just what you'll let her do and not do. The trick is to maintain a gentle but firm hand. Be kind, but don't let her manipulate you. You also can't lose your temper and make her feel small. If this goes the right way," she concluded, "you will find that in a few years, she'll have grown into an intelligent young woman who really does you proud," Josie told him.

The expression on his face told her that she hadn't convinced him. His words reaffirmed it. "That doesn't seem likely." He sounded sad about that—as if he wanted good things for his niece but wasn't sure they were possible.

"Don't doubt it," she stressed. "And don't ever make her feel that you're giving up on her. When you feel your temper going and you can't take any more, just step out. Count to ten—or a hundred if you have to—and then come back to start fresh," Josie advised. "I take it that she lives with you?"

"Yes. For now," he qualified.

She wanted to ask just how long "now" actually meant, but she sensed that he would think of that as prying, so she just continued as if he had answered the question she hadn't asked.

"This might be the most important 'now' in her young life."

He wondered if she was basing her thoughts on something in her recent experience with her own daughter.

Weighing whether or not to ask, he decided that at this point, what did he have to lose?

"You talk as if you've been through this," Declan said.

He couldn't quite interpret the quirky smile that curved her mouth. "I have."

"Your daughter," he guessed, remembering that she had mentioned having to raise the girl. He assumed that it was on her own, just like Peggy was doing. Declan couldn't help wondering if she had managed to do a better job than his sister had.

"My daughter," Josie confirmed.

"And she turned out all right?" he asked, even though he had had no intentions of burrowing into this woman's life, much less going this *far* into it. Somehow, what he wanted and what he actually did weren't one and the same thing.

The woman was a witch, he concluded. He had never acted so completely against type before.

"She turned out to be a strong young woman who knows her own mind and is on her way to becoming a doctor. I would like to see more of her and have her coming home summers, but she made her choices and I'm proud of her for sticking by them." Josie smiled at the instructor. "I'm sure you'll feel the same way about..." Her voice trailed off as she waited for Declan to fill in his niece's name.

"Shannon," he finally volunteered almost grudgingly. It astounded Declan that he had shared more with this woman in the space of less than an hour than he had with anyone in a long time, other than his mother. What was it about this Josie Whitaker that seemed to pull words out of his mouth even though he had no intentions of saying any of them?

"Shannon," she repeated, rolling the name around on her tongue as if she were literally savoring it. "That's a very pretty name."

Declan shrugged. He had no opinion one way or another about the girl's name. He hadn't even thought about it. "If you say so."

She had a feeling that he didn't make things any easier for the girl than his niece was apparently making things for him.

She wanted to ask him more questions. It was her nature to want to fix things. She knew if they stayed here talking, she would do just that. But she also wanted more lessons, so she knew that the smart thing to do was for her to back off. There was only one way for her to do that.

"Why don't you get back to those things you need to do? I can handle getting Marigold unsaddled and groomed from here," she told him.

Declan looked at her skeptically. "I thought you said you didn't know how." It was almost an accusation. Hadn't she asked him to talk her through it the first time?

"I have instincts," she told him. "I'm taking care of six-month-old twins."

"You have twins, too?" he questioned in surprise. Just how big a family did this woman have?

"My brother and sister-in-law do," she told him. "I came out here to help them out."

"All the way from Florida?" he questioned. But then, he'd rearranged his life for his mother and niece, also. That was just what family did.

He saw her wide smile. "You were listening, too," she said, pleased.

He didn't care for being caught, but he obviously had been. "Yeah, I was. Anyway, see that kid over there?" He pointed to where Steve Cartright was visible, mucking out one of the stalls. The high school boy boarded his horse with Declan and paid for it by working as a part-time stable hand, helping out as needed for an hour or two a day. Luckily, this was one of those times. "He'll walk you through unsaddling and brushing down Marigold. Come by the farmhouse and check with me before you leave," he instructed. "We'll make an appointment for your next lesson," he said as he walked out of the stable.

Chapter Four

Like everything else she undertook, Josie made certain that she did a good job taking care of Marigold. That meant going beyond just removing the mare's saddle with supervision from the boy who'd introduced himself as Steve.

She carefully uncinched the horse's saddle, took off the blanket beneath it and then removed the reins, bit and bridle, slipping the whole thing off.

"Well, you're free, girl, but I'm afraid that you still need to get cleaned up," she told Marigold, talking to the mare as if they were having a conversation. She ran her hand over the horse's rump. "I didn't ride you hard, but you still got pretty sweaty."

The mare turned her head, as if she were listening to every word Josie was saying and understood what she was being told. She even seemed to nod when Steve talked Josie through which brushes to use.

At least, she'd like to think so, Josie thought with a smile. But then, she had always felt like she could communicate with animals, whether they were big or small. That was one of the reasons she had also volunteered to spend her free time—if her time could actually be thought of as free—working with the dogs at Furever Paws, the local animal rescue.

Until recently, the shelter had been owned and operated by her aunts, affectionately known as "Bunny" and "Birdie," until the two sisters decided that, after all these years, they were ready to pass over management to someone else. Bunny had actually left town to tour the country in an RV with her secret beau, keeping in touch via phone calls. Birdie was still around but had taken a less active role once Rebekah had been hired to serve as the shelter's director.

Of course, things went a little topsy-turvy when Rebekah went on maternity leave, especially after the shelter's numbers shot through the roof after a whole slew of animals was rescued from a backyard breeder. Shelter operations had only just started calming down, thanks to the newly hired director— Bethany Robeson.

It only seemed logical to Josie that, since she was already in town to lend a hand to Rebekah and Grant with the twins, that hand should also be extended to include helping out at the animal shelter.

This was what Josie told the mare as she carefully groomed and brushed Marigold.

She continued talking because she noted that the sound of her voice seemed to soothe the animal. And, as for her…well, it just felt good to Josie to say all these things out loud. In a way, it actually helped to put her life in proper order.

"Well, we're done," she finally told the mare, with a quick glance over to Steve to confirm. Josie retired the brushes she had employed grooming the horse's coat. Finished, Josie stepped back to admire her work. "I don't mind telling you that you look exceptionally fetching, Marigold. You're probably going to have to fight off the other horses." She dropped her voice to a whisper and added, "Like that sexy stallion, Midnight."

Marigold whinnied as if she actually understood. It made Josie laugh.

"Yes, you know what I'm talking about, don't you, girl? Well, remember you can hold out if you want. Just because he's so big and powerful doesn't mean you have to fall at his feet at the first sign that he's interested in you." Josie grinned to herself as she wiped her hands off on the back of her jeans. Thankfully, Steve had moved on to other tasks so no one was listening. If they were, they would probably think she was talking about Declan. "Well, nice talking to you, Marigold. See you soon—I hope," she added.

She had no idea just how many lessons her brother and Rebekah had paid for. She doubted if it could be more than a couple. However, now that she had actually ridden a horse, making her lifelong dream come true, she was eager to do it again. This was despite the very sharp ache threatening to take over her back as well as her butt.

The latter was radiating pain with every step she took.

Making sure she had put away everything exactly where it belonged, Josie finally got into her car and drove the short distance over to the farmhouse.

She parked the vehicle close by, feeling it would be viewed as presumptuous of her if she parked it right in front of the house.

Not bothering to lock the car, Josie made her way over to the house and hurried up the front steps.

Josie knocked on the door then waited. And then knocked again.

At that point, she normally would have just left, but her unsmiling instructor had told her to let him know when she was leaving so he could tell her the time and date of their next riding. Josie was about to knock for a third time when the front door suddenly swung open.

Instead of looking up at the tall, muscular instructor the way she had expected, Josie found herself staring into the hostile green eyes of a rather gangly-looking redheaded fourteen-year-old girl. The teenager was scowling as she slowly took full measure of the woman standing on her doorstep.

"Yeah?" the girl finally asked.

There was no mistaking the challenge in the single word.

Rather than take offense at the teenager's attitude, Josie smiled at her. It wasn't hard to make the connection. "You must be Shannon."

A look of surprise crossed the girl's face. That was immediately followed by an even deeper scowl. "What of it?" the teen wanted to know. She gave every indication that she was spoiling for a fight.

In less than an instant, Josie was thrown back to Hannah's teen years. Her daughter had been really difficult to deal with back then, angry at her parents for their divorce, angry over her own feelings of abandonment, as well as having a whole host of other teenage angst-ridden issues that came wrapped up in their own packages.

No wonder Declan didn't smile, Josie thought. This was definitely a lot for the man to deal with, especially since, from what she had gathered, he had only recently taken temporary custody of the girl.

Josie did her best to make friends with the less than sunny teenager. "Your uncle told me a lot about you."

Shannon's frown only deepened. Her green eyes went dark. "I just bet he did," she answered sullenly. Shannon deliberately looked the woman on her doorstep up and down. "You his girlfriend?" she asked, her tone even less friendly than a moment ago.

The question caught Josie completely by surprise. But she managed to recover without expressing any sentiments that would give the teen any further ammunition. There wasn't even any sort of indication that the point-blank inquiry had managed to rattle her.

In a totally calm, friendly voice, Josie answered, "No, I'm his student."

The furrow between Shannon's brows deepened. "He's a teacher?" the teen questioned skeptically.

"Not the way you're probably thinking," Josie answered. "Your uncle is teaching me how to ride."

Shannon rolled her eyes then laughed shortly under her breath. The sound was far from friendly or even passably nice.

"He probably enjoys that," the girl told her. "Uncle Declan really likes bossing people around. It's kinda like his hobby."

Josie felt she needed to defend her instructor. It was easy to see that the man was in over his head. A lot of teenagers were really difficult to deal with at this stage of their lives.

"Maybe he just likes helping people and you're misunderstanding what he's telling you," Josie told the teenager.

A contemptuous look entered the girl's expressive green eyes. It was obvious that Shannon didn't think she was misunderstanding anything.

"You don't really believe that, do you?" the teenager challenged.

Josie's response had clearly caught Shannon off guard. "Actually, yes, I do," she told the teenager. Indicating the inside of the house beyond Shannon's shoulder, she asked, "May I come in?"

Shannon looked undecided for a second then shrugged her shoulders carelessly.

"You can do whatever you want," she told the

woman. After a beat, she opened the door further. "Doesn't matter to me what you do."

Letting the woman in, the teenager turned around for one parting shot. After that, she intended to hole up in what she thought of as a cubbyhole—the laughably small area that her grandmother had referred to as her room. But when Shannon looked, she saw her uncle's riding student smiling at her.

Shannon's back instantly went up. "What are you grinning about?" she queried.

"You," Josie answered easily.

That only made Shannon angrier. "Something funny about me?" Her tone was almost nasty as well as defensive.

"Oh no, there's nothing funny about you," Josie assured her. "You just remind me of someone."

The teenager made no secret that she was spoiling for a fight. "Who?" Shannon demanded, prepared to be on the receiving end of a derogatory remark.

"My daughter when she was your age," Josie told her easily. "No matter what I said, she always tried to turn it into a fight."

Shannon nodded knowingly. "So what did you do? Tell her to get her act together or you'd throw her out of the house?" Her mother had told her that more than once—when she had even acknowledged the fact that Shannon was around.

Shannon's guess told her a lot more than she was probably aware of, Josie thought.

The teen's bitter words wounded her heart. The girl had obviously been hurt and hurt badly. The first thing Josie thought of was that if Shannon was ever going to emerge out of this situation in one piece, the teen needed to be shown that her family cared about her and was there for her.

"No." Josie contradicted what Shannon had guessed. "I'd hug her—when she'd let me," she qualified. "And I'd tell her that no matter what she did or said, I would always love her."

The girl didn't look as if she believed her. "Did she laugh?" Shannon asked nastily.

"Well," Josie answered honestly, "it took her a while to come around and believe what I was telling her, but no, she didn't laugh."

Just at that moment, Champ, Declan's Australian shepherd came lumbering into the room. Josie noticed that her gangly adversary's eyes lit up for just a moment.

But the animal completely ignored both of them as it continued walking through the room, obviously looking for something or someone else.

The next moment, coming to and collecting herself, Shannon answered the question she assumed the woman had to be wondering.

"Champ's looking for my uncle. The dog follows him around like a shadow whenever he can. Champ's completely devoted to him." It wasn't hard to hear the wistfulness in the teenager's voice.

Josie nodded knowingly. An idea was forming in her head. "It's rough when a dog does that for someone else, especially when all you want is a little companionship," she acknowledged.

"I don't want anything," Shannon snapped. It was as if she refused to have a single warm emotion attributed to her.

"I was just speaking figuratively," Josie explained to the teen. Watching Shannon's face, she told the girl, "You know, I help out at an animal rescue a few times a week." She could see that she had caught the teenager's attention, at least for a moment. "They could always use some help if you're interested."

"I'm not," Shannon informed her, trying to make it sound as if she were an island unto herself. But then the façade cracked just a little as she asked, "What kind of animals?"

"All kinds," Josie answered easily. "Dogs and cats, mostly. They could all use a little love to help ease the way, until they find new homes."

Shannon shrugged, vainly doing her best to appear disinterested. But she failed. Her eyes gave her away, as did her tone of voice.

"I might be able to come to the shelter and help out sometime—if I'm not busy doing anything else."

Josie nodded. "That sounds great. If you decide you want to, I'll come by and pick you up," she told the teen. "That is, as long as it's all right with your uncle."

Shannon raised her chin defiantly. "Uncle Declan isn't the boss of me."

"I'm afraid that right now, he kind of is," Josie told her. She could see that her words weren't exactly warming the girl's heart. But she wasn't through trying to get through to Shannon. "You know, your uncle really does care about you."

"Oh yeah, sure," Shannon answered sarcastically. "Like I believe that."

But Josie refused to give up and back down. "You should, you know." The defiant look on the teen's face only intensified. Josie decided to approach this from another angle, talking to the teenager as if she were sharing a confidence. "You should know that men have difficulty showing what they're really feeling. They think it makes them look weak," she told the girl. "But that doesn't change the fact that they really do feel things. And that they care," Josie emphasized. And then she leaned in to share a "secret."

"I do know that sometimes they can drive you up the wall. There are times when you'll be so annoyed, you'll want to scream. Trust me, we've all been there."

Josie saw Shannon's eyes light up again. She had obviously struck pay dirt, she thought. For a moment, the girl seemed to forget all about playing the bored, disinterested teenager.

"For real?" she asked.

"For real," Josie answered solemnly.

The grin she saw on the teenager's face was wide and looked genuine.

Finally, Josie thought, silently celebrating that they had had a breakthrough of sorts. The rest of the journey should be easier.

Declan picked this moment to walk in on the temporary truce. Surprised to see his student, there was no mistaking the annoyed look that he sent in his niece's direction.

"Nobody told me you were here," he said to Josie. His accusation was obvious.

"I just walked in," Josie said, trying to placate the cowboy and cover for Shannon. "And I was just in the process of explaining to your niece who I was. She was leery of letting in a stranger," she added, hoping that gave the girl points in his eyes. "Marigold's all cleaned up and put away," Josie concluded, turning the conversation away from his niece.

Declan cast a glance in Shannon's direction. "At least someone does what I ask them to," he commented, referring to his student, not his niece.

Josie could see the teenager begin to rise to the bait. The scowl was back. That meant an explosion couldn't be that far behind. She couldn't allow that to happen.

"Mr. Hoyt, could I speak to you for a moment?" Josie requested.

Declan saw no need for privacy, but he had no desire to have a conversation around Shannon right now either. The girl took everything he said and somehow found a way to irritate him beyond belief.

"Sure," he answered. "You can follow me to the kitchen."

In the kitchen, he turned around so abruptly, he almost succeeded in bumping into Josie. "Okay, what is it you want to say?"

"I have a proposition for you," she told him.

"Oh?" At this point, he had no idea what to expect, only that he probably wouldn't like it.

Once again the conversation didn't turn out the way he'd expected.

"You obviously could use a little help dealing with Shannon. How about if I offer to supply that help to you?" Josie asked.

Nothing was free, Declan thought. He braced himself. "In exchange for what?" he wanted to know.

"A few more riding lessons," Josie answered. "I'm sure my brother and sister-in-law only paid for a few."

"Two lessons actually," he confirmed.

"All right. Let's up the ante to five lessons in all. Five lessons and I'll come by three, four times a week—maybe more—to take your niece to the Furever Paws animal shelter to help out there. She expressed a keen interest in working with the animals and—"

He didn't need to hear any more. Shannon needed something to keep her occupied, and this sounded like it could be a perfect fit. Declan put his hand out to her. "You've got yourself a deal, Miss Whitaker," he told her.

"Josie," she corrected.

He nodded. "Josie," he echoed.

This had been easier than she had thought it would be. The man was obviously desperate.

She smiled as they shook on it.

Chapter Five

The deal was struck.

Because of Declan's busy workload, arrangements for her next riding lesson were set for the same time the following week. Her schedule was no less hectic, but Josie intended to take the man's niece to the animal shelter much sooner than that.

For one thing, she didn't think that either Declan or Shannon could last another week in each other's company without this sort of diversion for the girl. It was obvious to Josie that something was needed to defuse the situation and get Shannon involved in something where she could put her energy to good use and actually feel as if she was being useful.

Everyone needed to feel useful, she thought.

All in all, Josie was in good spirits when she returned to her brother's house. Instead of going to the tiny apartment that had been set up for her above the garage, she walked into the main house.

The first person she ran into was Rebekah. With the twins appearing to be mercifully asleep for a short duration of time, her sister-in-law was attempting to catch up on housework.

Everywhere she looked, Josie could tell that something needed doing. Twins generated a huge amount of housework—more laundry, more garbage, more *stuff* everywhere, ranging from changing tables to toys to diaper pails, cluttering up the house and getting in the way, making it hard to keep things tidy. It never really felt like they were fully caught up.

Rebekah brightened just a little when she saw her sister-in-law come in.

"How did it go?" she wanted to know.

"Very well. I didn't fall off the horse once," Josie answered cheerfully. She looked around. There was just the two of them in the kitchen. "Are the babies asleep?" she asked.

Rebekah nodded. Josie thought that the young woman really looked beyond tired.

"Yes, Virginia, there is a Santa Claus," Rebekah said, smiling wearily.

"I've got an idea. Why don't you take advantage of the downtime, Bekah?" Josie gestured toward the doorway leading to the stairs. "Go and take a nap. I know it's been a rough couple of days with that cold you and the twins all got."

"I can't. There's just too much to do," Rebekah lamented, looking at the mess surrounding them.

Rather than argue with her sister-in-law, Josie took the dish towel out of Rebekah's hands. The latter didn't try very hard to hold on to it.

"I'll take care of it all," Josie promised. "All I want you to do is get some sleep before you officially become a zombie."

"But—" It sounded like a halfhearted protest at best.

"Don't argue with me," Josie told the young woman. "I'm here to help, remember? So let me help."

Unable to muster the energy to offer a proper protest, Rebekah gave in. "I just need five minutes," she said as she began to walk toward the family room sofa.

"Forget about five minutes," she told her sister-in-law. "Take as much time as you need," Josie ordered as she continued to wash the dishes that Rebekah had just turned her attention away from.

The latter stopped in the doorway for a moment to smile her thanks. "You're a saint, Josie."

Josie nodded solemnly. "There's been some talk about canonizing me," she quipped before a smile cracked her straight face.

"I'll be the first one in line to sign the petition," Rebekah promised just as she left the room.

Josie chuckled to herself.

With quick, efficient movements, she went from one outstanding chore to the next, deftly finishing each. She was more than happy to be able to do this for her brother and sister-in-law. Not only because she really liked them, but because it allowed her to relive and remember her own time that had been spent trying to work and take care of her house while also attempting to raise her daughter at the same time.

She also remembered that it had always felt as if she'd had to let something go. Usually, that meant not taking care of her daughter herself because she could always find friends who were willing to pitch in, young mothers who would take Hannah with them while caring for their own kids.

The recollection pained her. With any luck, Josie thought, Rebekah wouldn't have to feel that way.

Working quickly, Josie managed to get a great deal done before the plaintive cries of one of the twins—Lily if she didn't miss her guess—floated through the air, signaling that her nap was over.

Drying her hands, Josie went to the nursery to see to the needs of at least one of the twins before it became both of them.

The following morning was one of her days to volunteer at the shelter. Before going, Josie decided to call Shannon to see if the teenager wanted to go with her. Who knew, maybe she was busy or had changed her mind about coming along.

"Yeah, I want to go," Shannon instantly blurted out in answer to the question. Josie could almost see the girl beaming as she talked to her on the phone.

"You're going to have to check with your uncle," Josie reminded the teenager. "To make sure it's all right with him and that he doesn't have anything for you to do before you go."

"He doesn't care what I do," Shannon insisted, but Josie could hear the tension in her voice.

She was afraid of being told no, Josie thought. "Shannon, you still need to check with him. Your uncle is responsible for you," she reminded the girl. "At the very least, you need to tell your uncle Declan that you're going to the shelter with me."

Josie heard a huge, impatient sigh on the other end of the line.

"All right, all right," Shannon answered. "You are coming for me, right?" the teenager asked her uncertainly.

"I'm leaving right now," Josie told the girl. She picked up her purse by the door then hurried down the stairs of her over-the-garage apartment.

"Great. I'll be ready. And yes," Shannon added quickly, anticipating what the woman was going to tell her, "don't worry, I'll let Uncle Declan know."

"Very good," Josie said.

She knew that if she praised the girl at all, she needed to be very careful how she voiced her approval. As much as Shannon probably needed affirmation, Josie appreciated that teenagers like Shannon could be very touchy. One sentiment incorrectly stated and everything could very easily fall apart.

Feeling extremely good about this whole endeavor

with Shannon that she was undertaking, Josie turned up the music as she drove to her destination.

Reaching the farmhouse, Josie didn't even have time to park her car. It was obvious that Shannon had been watching and waiting for her, peering through the front window. The moment that Josie had pulled up, Shannon threw open the door and came flying down the front steps.

Opening up the passenger's-side door, Shannon hopped into her seat.

"Okay, let's go!" she declared, hardly able to contain herself.

Josie definitely wanted to get on the girl's good side. However, she couldn't help being a bit suspicious about the display of anxious readiness to take off like this.

Rather than pull out, Josie turned off her engine.

"Why aren't we going?" Shannon demanded in an accusing voice.

Josie shifted in her seat to face the girl. "Did you tell your uncle that you were going?" she asked Shannon.

"I said I would, didn't I?" the girl challenged Josie.

"Yes. Yes, you did," Josie acknowledged. However she wasn't all that certain that she could take the teenager's word for it.

"Then let's go," the girl urged.

Keeping her voice as friendly as possible, Josie asked, "If you don't mind my asking, why are you in such a hurry to leave?"

Shannon made no bones about pouting as she answered. "Because I'm afraid Uncle Declan will change his mind and find something for me to do instead."

"And that's the only reason?" Josie asked, carefully looking at the teenager's face.

"Yes," Shannon all but bit off.

Josie weighed the teenager's expression against her gut instinct. "Okay then, let's go," she said, starting up the engine again.

"Wait, you believe me?" the teenager asked, obviously surprised.

"Well," Josie answered, choosing her words carefully, "you said you told your uncle you were coming with me to the animal shelter, and I know that he thinks that's a good idea, so yes, I believe you."

The girl pressed her lips together, as if debating whether or not to say something.

The internal argument she was having was short-lived and she decided to be completely honest about the situation.

"Wait. I didn't say anything—exactly," Shannon admitted.

"Oh? What did you do? 'Exactly,'" Josie questioned, emphasizing the single word.

"I wrote him a note saying I was going with you to the animal shelter. I left it on the kitchen table," she said, each word dribbling from her lips almost in slow motion. She slanted her eyes toward Josie. "That's okay, isn't it?"

"Is the note where he can see it?" Josie asked.

"Yeah, I said it was on the kitchen table." Shannon's voice was almost defensive.

Josie wanted to give Declan a quick call just to be certain that the girl had left the note out in plain sight, but she knew that if she did that, it would be a blunt statement that she didn't trust Shannon. This trip to the shelter was the very first step in their brand-new friendship.

She didn't want to risk blowing it all up before the relationship had a chance to even get started.

"Yes, you did," Josie replied. "I just wanted to make sure that your uncle knew where you had gone so he wouldn't worry about you."

The familiar unappreciative scowl was back on Shannon's face. She shrugged her shoulders, dismissing what Josie had just said. "I did all the chores he gave me, so he's not going to worry about where I am."

Her heart went out to the teenager. It was awful if she really believed what she was saying. "Oh, honey, you're all wrong about your uncle. He might sound gruff, but he loves you and he does worry."

It was obvious by her expression that Shannon didn't believe her. "I'm not a little girl. You don't have to make things up on my account."

"I know that you're not a little girl and I'm not making anything up. I really don't think you give your uncle enough credit. If he was as uncaring as you seem to think he is, he would have had Children's Services come and pick you up instead of taking you in."

Shannon felt she had an explanation for that. "That's just because my mom's in rehab and there was nowhere else for me to go. My grandma and grandpa used to take me in when my mother had one of her sprees. But then Grandpa died and Grandma moved in with Uncle Declan, so now we're stuck with each other," Shannon grumbled.

"Yes, but that didn't mean that he automatically had to take you in, too," she noted gently.

"Sure he did," Shannon insisted. "Grandma would have given him hell if he hadn't."

She looked at the teenager, certain that the girl knew better than that. "If your uncle was as uncaring as you seem to believe, upsetting his mother wouldn't matter to him. C'mon, Shannon. Give the poor man a break. After all, he's obviously trying to give you one," Josie pointed out.

In Josie's opinion, Shannon looked as if she were wavering. The teenager sighed. "Yeah, okay. Maybe I should call him," she said.

Josie reached over and took her cell phone out from the container she had for it on her dashboard. Handing the phone to the girl, she said, "Go ahead, be my guest. Call your uncle."

Shannon looked at her, appearing a little uneasy, then gazed back at the phone. "Yeah, right," she murmured. "My uncle." She raised her eyes, looking at Josie. "I did leave that note for him, you know," she said defensively.

"I know. I just thought that you might want to tell him where you were going in person, but if you'd rather just go with the note you left, that's fine," Josie told her. "As long as he knows where you are, that's all that matters. I just didn't want anything to be on your mind and interfering with you enjoying all those cuddly puppies and kittens at the shelter."

Shannon frowned, as if registering her displeasure. But nonetheless, she began dialing her uncle's phone number.

The phone on the other end rang and she counted off the number of rings. When his voice mail picked up, the teenager confided to Josie, "His voice mail sounds just as grumpy as Uncle Declan in real life." Removing her hand, the teenager went on to talking into the phone. "Uncle Declan, this is Shannon. Josie stopped by the house and I'm going with her to the animal shelter. I left you a note, but Josie thought you might miss the note, so I'm calling to let you know." Glancing at Josie, she added, "In case you get worried."

With that, she peeked at Josie quizzically, the look in her eyes silently asking the woman if there was anything else she needed to add.

Josie gave her a thumbs-up, letting her know that she had done fine.

Shannon terminated the call and handed the phone back to Josie.

"Next stop, the animal shelter," Josie announced. There was a touch of anticipation in her voice.

Josie saw that the girl was shifting in her seat, as if she couldn't bring herself to sit still. Shannon was obviously excited about going to the animal shelter, she thought. Josie was tickled by the girl's anticipation of the event.

"Is there anything I should know or, you know, do when we get to the shelter?" Shannon wanted to know. She was eager not to make any mistakes right off the bat.

"Well…" She thought for a moment. "Just don't let all those dogs overwhelm you," Josie warned. "Some of the dogs are a little rough and others are overly eager. Last time I was there, I saw that a couple of the new dogs were big enough to knock you over, but you can definitely see them coming and brace yourself. Most of the dogs are just eager for affection."

"Affection," Shannon repeated. The expression on her face said that she knew what that was like. "I can handle that," she told Josie.

"I'm sure you can," Josie assured her. And then she smiled. "This is going to be fun," Josie promised.

Chapter Six

And it was fun.

The moment Josie walked into the animal shelter with Shannon, she could see that the teenager was completely captivated with the various different types of dogs that had been given temporary homes there. Mesmerized, the teenager didn't know where to look first.

"Where did they all come from?" Shannon wanted to know.

"Some were abandoned, some were found wandering the streets, a few were handed in by their owners because the owners were too old or too infirmed or too poor to take care of them properly any longer. There was a sad case a few weeks back where the authorities found out about a backyard breeding operation. When they went to shut it down, they found the dogs in pretty bad shape. This little lady," Josie said, bending down to remove one cockapoo puppy, Harlow, that had sunk her teeth into the hem of Shannon's jeans, "was part of that group."

The five-month-old cockapoo wiggled to get free once Josie managed to separate the puppy's teeth from the bottom of her jeans.

"Want to hold her?" Josie asked, holding the puppy out to Shannon.

"Can I?" She seemed barely able to contain herself.

The puppy leaned over toward her as far as she could while still in Josie's arms. Her little pink tongue flicked over Shannon's cheek.

"I think you have your answer," Josie laughed.

The transformation was almost breathtakingly quick. In amazingly short order, Shannon ceased being the belligerent teenager with a giant chip on her shoulder and transformed into a soft, caring young teenager who just wanted to help take care of, and in some cases help socialize, the dogs—puppies and full grown alike—that had only recently been brought in to the shelter.

As Josie watched, she saw Shannon's better qualities emerge. Displaying a patience Josie was certain that the girl's uncle had no idea she possessed, the teen began drawing out not only the newly found puppies but some of the older dogs as well.

It was amazing to watch.

Josie could see that a number of animals took to Shannon. The teen certainly took to them. In one instance, Shannon managed to coax an undersized German shepherd out of the corner where she was hiding. Audrey, which was what they had named her at the shelter, seemed to try to all but withdraw into herself. It was as if the poor thing were attempting to "melt" out of sight.

Without any prompting from Josie, Shannon began talking to Audrey in a soft, gentle, soothing voice. The teenager made no sudden moves toward the dog, she just kept on talking until she could get the rather small German shepard to leave the corner where she was attempting to hide. It took a few more minutes before Audrey became brave enough to move a little closer toward the teenager.

After what seemed like an eternity, the dog allowed Shannon to finally stroke her. Shannon was fairly beaming as she glanced up at Josie.

"Look, Josie, I think she likes me," Shannon said in a low voice, calling the woman's attention to what was happening. The teen had managed to get the dog to respond to her.

"Oh, I know she does. Nobody else has been able to get near her like that, and you just managed to do it in under an hour," Josie told the girl, extremely pleased.

"Really?" Shannon asked, thrilled at her own accomplishment. She felt a sort of pride that she had never experienced before. It was as if she had found her calling.

"Really," Josie assured the teen.

Eventually, she realized that they had been there a long time. Glancing at her watch, Josie saw what time it was. As much as she hated taking Shannon away, she knew that she should be getting the girl back. Not only that, but she needed to be getting back to Grant and Rebekah. She knew they wouldn't say anything to her, but she had been gone for close to four hours and Rebekah was probably in need of a break.

"I'm afraid we're going to have to be getting back, Shannon," she told the girl.

"Can't we stay just a little while longer?" Shannon begged. Josie thought that the teen looked as if she was prepared to go on petting the puppy she currently had in her arms for hours.

"I'd really love to, honey. But in addition to volunteering here at the shelter, I am also helping out my brother and sister-in-law take care of their twins. Lily and Lucas are still little itty-bitty things, but they have really powerful lungs. I'm pitching in to help until they at least get a little bigger." She looked at the teenager, hoping the girl understood.

Shannon reluctantly nodded and got to her feet. She looked at the puppy wistfully. "Can we come back some time?"

"Oh absolutely," Josie promised.

The teenager pressed her lips together then hesitantly asked, "Soon?"

Josie had no intention of drawing this out. That would be cruel. It was obvious that the teenager enjoyed working with the animals, especially this last bunch.

"How does the day after tomorrow sound?" Josie asked the girl.

"Tomorrow sounds better," Shannon countered, watching Josie's face hopefully.

"I can't come tomorrow," she told Shannon. "I've got other responsibilities. But the day after definitely sounds doable. Unless you're busy, of course," Josie said tongue-in-cheek.

"No, not busy at all. The day after tomorrow sounds great," Shannon said enthusiastically.

"Is ten o'clock enough time for you to do your chores first?"

Shannon looked somewhat less than thrilled to be reminded about the chores her uncle had her doing, but she answered Josie's question without hesitation. "More than enough time. I can be finished by nine if I get up early."

That, Josie surmised, was Shannon's plan.

Josie nodded. "Then I'll be at your house at nine to pick you up," she promised. She was rewarded by an exceptionally wide smile from Shannon.

Slipping her arm around the girl's shoulders as they left the shelter, Josie told her, "You did a great job today."

Shannon looked really surprised by Josie's declaration. It seemed like she wasn't accustomed to being on the receiving end of a compliment, or any sort of positive feedback, really.

"I did?" she asked, her eyes widening.

"Absolutely. Bethany Robeson, that's the shelter's director," she said, mentioning the name of the newly hired director, "was very impressed with you," Josie told the teenager. The woman had come by, as was her habit, to check on the volunteers. "She wanted to know if you were going to come by again to work with the dogs, particularly the shier ones."

Shannon's eyes were sparkling now. "She did? What did you say?" she asked eagerly.

"I told her that you were. She wanted me to let you know that you're welcome to come by the shelter any time. She said that the shelter could really use more people like you," she added, knowing that everyone liked and needed approval.

Josie noticed that the girl was walking on air by the time they got to her car in the parking lot.

She remembered how tough this age had been for Hannah, how much she'd craved affirmation. Hannah hadn't always been willing to accept it from Josie— usually replying with "You have to say that because you're my mom"—but if Josie could mention some teacher or mentor who'd pointed out how well Hannah was doing, her daughter would beam for days. Thankfully, they'd finally gotten to a good place in their relationship where compliments didn't have to come secondhand. Josie slipped out her cell phone and sent her daughter a quick text, just letting her know how proud she was of her. Hannah must have seen it right away, because she soon tagged it with a heart. And now Josie was the one who couldn't stop smiling.

All in all, she thought as she got into her vehicle, this had been a very successful undertaking.

Working with the dogs was good for Shannon and Shannon was apparently good for the dogs, too.

"She really said that?" Shannon questioned happily, wanting to hear the words again.

"She did indeed," Josie assured the teenager.

Belatedly, Shannon got into the car on the passenger side and settled back in her seat. Snapping her seat belt, she looked at the older woman. "Josie?"

"Yes?" Josie asked, not really knowing what she was about to hear.

"Thanks for bringing me."

The words were almost mumbled. It was obvious that this wasn't a common thing for the teenager to say, which was why it meant even more to Josie.

Smiling at Shannon, Josie replied, "Thanks for coming."

And just like that, the floodgates burst open and Shannon began asking all sorts of questions about some of the various dogs she had encountered at the shelter. The girl sounded, Josie thought, like a regular teenager—a happier one than the one she had first met.

Josie couldn't help hoping that the girl's uncle wouldn't inadvertently do or say anything that would wind up raining on Shannon's little parade.

True to her word, Josie came by two days later at exactly nine o'clock to pick Shannon up and take the teenager back to the animal shelter. Shannon told her that the pickup time was going to have to change.

Her uncle was enrolling her in high school and she wouldn't be home until after three.

"But I still want to help out at the shelter," Shannon stressed eagerly.

"I'll see about changing my hours around," Josie promised.

Shannon beamed.

The girl enjoyed herself even more than she had the first time she had gone to the shelter. A little more familiar with the way the shelter operated now, Shannon was less self-conscious. The teen seemed to feel that much more secure in approaching and working with the puppies.

A new batch had been found on the street and brought in just the day before. Shannon took an active part in socializing the puppies.

Josie was very happy that the teenager could work without needing any sort of close supervision. The girl, Josie thought, was a natural. Shannon truly seemed to have found her niche. Socializing the puppies brought out the absolute best in the girl.

Josie could notice the change in the teenager immediately. She wondered if Declan would as well.

It would definitely give them something to talk about when she came for her second lesson, Josie mused. Of course, the lesson was still several days away. She couldn't wait, even though she knew she had a lot to get done before then.

Her life was extremely busy and chock-full of work from one end to the other. Helping out with the twins took up a lot of her time, plus she also made an effort to get involved in the community, including making friends with Grant and Rebekah's neighbors and unloading her baking on everyone in a five-mile radius. Back in Florida, she'd run a catering business, and cooking—most especially baking—had become her default way to de-stress and work through her thoughts. She couldn't get out of the habit, and now she'd earned a reputation for being the one to bring over a pie to a neighbor sick at home, or to make brownies as a treat for a three-year-old's birthday. With all of that, plus volunteering at the shelter, when it came to the riding lessons, Josie felt as if the days were just dragging themselves by one frozen second at a time. Getting to the following week for her second lesson felt as if it was taking forever.

But finally, at long last, that day arrived.

Full of anticipation and eager to get started, Josie arrived early.

Declan was nowhere to be seen, either in the stable or at the corral. But to her surprise, Shannon was there. The girl had obviously gone out of her way to stop by at the stable.

Shannon didn't even pretend to be surprised to see the woman she now thought of as a friend.

"You here to see my uncle?" she wanted to know. There was a trace of curiosity with a little underlying suspicion in her voice.

"Not directly," Josie told the girl. She definitely didn't want the girl thinking there was anything romantic going on between Declan and herself. "I'm here for my riding lesson. Your uncle said he could give me my second lesson today."

Josie looked around the area, but there was no sign of the man. She should have called to confirm, Josie thought, disappointed.

"You don't think he's forgotten, do you?" she asked Shannon.

It would be a little awkward, Josie thought, hanging around the stable if Declan turned out to be occupied elsewhere and didn't come. She really should have called. Josie upbraided herself.

"Uncle Declan doesn't forget anything. Ever," Shannon told her, emphasizing the last word.

Josie wasn't sure if Shannon meant that as a criticism or was just stating a fact she found annoying for some reason.

"Then I guess he'll be here," Josie said.

The words were no sooner out of her mouth than she saw the handsome cowboy crossing the field and walking toward them.

"And there he is," Shannon told her, pointing to her uncle. Instead of making herself scarce, Shannon started talking quickly. "I just wanted to tell you that I had a great time helping you the other day."

The deep sincerity in Shannon's voice made Josie smile. "You weren't helping me, you were helping the animals at the shelter," she pointed out tactfully.

"Can we do it again tomorrow?" Shannon asked eagerly just as Declan reached them.

"I'd love that," Josie answered then told her, "I'll be by to pick you up at the same time."

"Cool." Shannon's smile grew wider. With that

one parting word, she made her way past her uncle, still keeping her smile in place. And then she headed back toward the house.

"You ready for your second lesson?" Declan asked by way of a greeting, skipping right over any sort of a salutation.

"Absolutely," Josie answered.

She made no effort to hide the eager enthusiasm in her voice. She had actually dreamed about riding last night. She vaguely remembered that Declan had been in the dream somewhere, but the part that had really caught her attention was that she was riding through a field with the wind in her hair. It had felt very liberating.

"All right. This time you're going to saddle your horse, too," Declan told her.

"Is my horse still going be Marigold?" Josie wanted to know. She followed Declan into the stable, mentally crossing her fingers that he would say yes.

He glanced over his shoulder. "You want another horse?"

"Oh no," Josie answered a little too quickly. "I really like Marigold. She's a very gentle horse. It's almost as if she can sense what I'm feeling."

"All right, then it's settled. You're riding the same horse. If something works," Declan told her, espousing one of his more strongly held beliefs, "don't try to mess with it."

"My sentiments exactly," Josie told her instructor. She knew better than to smile. The man might get the idea that she was having fun at his expense, and she really wasn't.

Declan bought her over to the far stall. Midnight stood waiting to be saddled as well. Both horses were located next to one another.

Declan saw the quizzical expression on Josie's face. "I figured we could saddle our horses together."

She knew what he wasn't saying. That if she had any questions, she could get them answered just by observing what he was doing.

She noticed that Declan had already placed both her saddle and his on the upper edge of the stall. Both were within easy access. Blankets and bridles were there as well, next to the saddles.

The next moment, Declan was getting started without so much as saying a word to her.

Josie quickly positioned the blanket then hefted the saddle. It seemed heavier lifting than removing it, she noticed. Silently telling herself not to drop the saddle, she placed the saddle on top of the blanket. Successful, she carefully tightened the cinch beneath Marigold's belly, sneaking a look over at Declan. He was watching, and he hadn't said anything to stop her, so she assumed that meant she was doing it right.

Satisfied that the saddle would remain in place, Josie went on to put the bridle on, getting the bit in place and then easing the crown of the bridle over the mare's ears.

Finished, Josie turned around to see that Declan had already finished saddling his horse well ahead of her.

Their eyes met. Declan nodded at her.

"Good," he said.

The single word of praise felt almost heady to Josie. She instinctively knew how rarely he bothered with it.

"All right, let's go out," he told her, leading Midnight from the stable and into the corral.

Josie did as he said. She fully expected that she would be mounting her horse once they were out in the corral. But Declan turned toward her and surprised Josie by giving her a compliment. Not about the way she had saddled her horse. The praise he uttered revolved around her treatment of his niece.

"You realize that you worked a miracle with Shannon," he told her.

Taken completely aback, Josie looked at her instructor and blinked. She had probably just misheard. "Excuse me?"

"The kid's been walking on air since you brought her back from that animal shelter. She's been waiting for you to come by from the minute she finished her chores. And that's another thing," he went on, mounting his horse. "I don't have to get on her case to do her chores. She actually does them first thing right after she gets up. Of course," he continued with a shrug, "she's still complaining about the slow internet signal her phone's been getting, but I guess you can't have everything."

Mounting Marigold, Josie had to bite back a laugh. She didn't want Declan thinking that she was laughing at him. "No, I guess you can't."

"Don't see why teenagers are so attached to the damn things anyway," he complained. He had no use for phones in general, much less one that did all the fancy things he'd read about.

"It's their way of communicating," she tried to explain to Declan.

He snorted dismissively. "You ask me, sitting down and having a healthy conversation with someone who's in the same room as you should be good enough for them." He had even had a few of those conversations with Shannon lately. He found himself looking forward to having more.

"When you're lonely," she told him, "it can be nice to know that you can reach out to someone else and get a response," she explained.

"Well then, they should find something to occupy themselves. You can't be lonely if you're busy," Declan told her. Before she could say anything in response, he changed the topic. "You want to go ride out to the meadow?"

The thought of going on a longer ride than they had during their first lesson immediately caught her attention. "I'd love it."

"Then let's go," he told her.

The words were no sooner out of Declan's mouth than he kicked his horse's flanks and took off.

Caught off guard, it took a moment for Josie's competitive spirit to kick in. She found that she had to really hustle in order to keep up with her instructor and not fall behind.

She found it incredibly exhilarating.

Chapter Seven

Josie's heart was pounding fast and hard by the time Declan finally pulled up on Midnight's reins and brought the horse to a full halt.

Even at Marigold's fastest speed, Josie found herself trailing a few steps behind Declan and totally exhausted. She was more than ready for the ride—or race as it had turned into—to come to a stop.

Managing to bring her horse almost right beside Declan's stallion, Josie was desperately trying to catch her breath.

Even so, it took her more than a few moments to be able to say anything mildly coherent. Her breathing was still coming in snatches.

The first thing Declan noticed when he looked at her was that the woman's complexion was glowing.

In his opinion, his student looked rather alluring. Her hair had come partially undone from the bun she had initially fashioned. There were tendrils all around her face.

He caught himself thinking that Josie looked positively radiant and sexy.

The silence, coupled with her heavy breathing, made Declan feel a little awkward. Normally, silence didn't bother him. He actually invited it. But for some reason, it bothered him this time.

He needed to say *something*, Declan thought. "I was afraid I was going to lose you," he finally told her as he dismounted. It wasn't exactly a scintillating revelation, but at least he had managed to banish the silence.

Josie remained exactly where she was. Truthfully, she was afraid to make a move. At the moment, her back and legs felt much too stiff, thanks to being jostled. She felt that dismounting gracefully right now might prove to be way too much of a challenge.

"No such luck," she replied, trying her best to speak in a natural cadence.

Declan made his way over to his student and her mount.

"Are you planning on getting off sometime soon?" he asked. "Or do you just enjoy looking down at me?"

"I'm going to get off," she told him. About to make an attempt to do so, she felt a cramp suddenly dance down her leg. "Soon," she added after a moment.

He caught the hesitation in her voice. "Something wrong?" Declan wanted to know, studying her.

"No, of course not," Josie denied a little too quickly.

"All right, then let's see you come down," he told her.

It was more of a challenge than a simple instruction. He was beginning to think that for some reason, Josie *couldn't* dismount. If there was some sort of a problem, he wanted to know, although for the life of him, he couldn't guess what it was.

"All right," she answered.

Josie didn't make the attempt to dismount immediately. Still, she knew she couldn't remain just sitting on her mare like this. She certainly didn't want to explain to Declan that her legs felt incredibly wobbly, even more than they had the first time she had ridden on the horse. Most likely he would just think that she was making up excuses.

Maybe her legs weren't as bad as she thought, Josie told herself. Maybe this was all in her head.

"Josie?" he questioned.

Declan had no idea what to make of the woman's inertia. According to his niece, who seemed to actually be sharing things with him lately, Josie never stopped moving. Yet here the woman was, all but frozen in place. Was there really something wrong, or had she just decided that she had had enough of riding and didn't know how to tell him because of the bargain they had struck regarding more lessons in exchange for her working with Shannon? He readily admitted that he wasn't exactly the easiest man to talk to.

"I'm getting off," Josie told him, anticipating Declan's next question. "I was just noticing how beautiful everything looks from up here."

It was the only thing she could think of to try to distract him and get his mind off her inability to dismount.

"The scenery is just as beautiful from the ground," he told her.

What did she expect him to say? "You're absolutely right," she agreed.

Holding on to the saddle horn, Josie bit down on her lower lip and swung her leg up over the horse's rump. Her leg felt as if it weighed at least twenty pounds heavier. Maneuvering it was far from easy, but she refused to look helpless in front of Declan. Being helpless went against everything she believed in.

As she brought down her other leg, Josie could feel both legs weakening. She was sinking for just a split second. And then she felt Declan's arms tightening around her.

Rather than setting her on the ground the way she expected, Declan continued holding her against him.

"I'm beginning to think that you've come up with your own rather unique way of dismounting," he told her, a hint of amusement curving his mouth.

"I guess maybe I did ride Marigold a little too hard," she admitted.

He looked the horse over from his vantage point.

"Well, Marigold doesn't seem to be any the worse for it," he commented.

"Why should she be? Marigold outweighs me," Josie told him.

"I didn't take you for the type who would be making excuses," Declan told her.

"I'm not making excuses," Josie protested. "I'm just making observations."

Declan nodded. The rare, elusive smile on his lips intensifying just a shade.

"Speaking of observations…" he said. "You were fairly flying on Marigold. Lucky for both of us that she didn't come to an unexpected, sudden stop. She's been known to do that on occasion when she's been ridden harder than she's accustomed to," Declan told her. Not that he had thought that would be a problem when it came to Josie, since he'd assumed she'd take it slow. He supposed that he had misjudged the woman. "I wouldn't want to see you landing on your head."

Josie laughed. "Good thing you didn't have to come to my rescue," she quipped.

"Yeah, good thing," he echoed, very aware that his arms were still around Josie, holding her fairly close to him.

The warm breeze was wrapping itself around both of them. Declan had to admit that he felt this strong, overwhelming desire just to tilt Josie's head back and bring his lips down on hers.

His reaction wasn't because of anything that she had done, he realized. It was just her. He was at-

tracted to her. There was something about her, a can-
do spirit that spoke to him, that just pulled him in.

And, if he were being honest about this, Josie was
being almost annoyingly distant around him. Even
though they had just been literally thrown together—
and not for the first time—Josie had made absolutely
no attempt to move in on him.

She hadn't even flirted with him.

If anything, she was treating him as if he was her
younger brother. He definitely wasn't accustomed to
being discounted in this manner. On the contrary,
every one of the women who approached him for
riding lessons would, at some point or other, make
advances, attempting to stir him up in some fashion.

Some had even flirted with him outrageously.

He had always taken it as a challenge not to react
in any way to any of those women. The reason for
that was because he didn't want the lines between
his riding student and him to blur.

For the very first time in his life, Declan found
that he was willing to allow those lines to get blurry.
To his surprise, it was Josie who seemed determined
that they each stay in their separate lanes and not mix
pleasure with business.

"Um, I think you can let go of me now," Josie
prompted.

Declan looked rather skeptically into her eyes.
"Are you sure you're not going to fall down if I do?"
he wanted to know.

No, she wasn't sure, but she was determined to
remain upright. "I'm sure," she answered firmly.

He nodded, but rather than remove his arms, Declan only loosened his hold on her.

"I think it wouldn't be such a bad idea if you just sat for a little bit," he told her. Seeing the hesitancy in her face, Declan added, "Tell you what, I'll even join you."

Holding Josie's hand, Declan lowered himself to the ground. He carefully drew her down beside him.

"I really am okay," Josie assured her riding instructor. The last thing she wanted was for Declan to think of her as some sort of fragile, hothouse flower.

"It still wouldn't hurt for you to sit," he said, looking at her.

Her heart was beginning to settle down, the effects of her exhilarating ride fading until they were totally manageable.

Sitting next to him, Josie found herself extremely aware of Declan. There was no denying that the man was more than just attractive—very attractive, she amended—but she couldn't allow herself to respond to him in any way.

There were reasons for that.

She felt she was just too old for him. Shannon had mentioned that he was thirty-eight, which meant there were six years between them. She had been married and had her family. Granted that family only included her daughter, a daughter who was now fully grown and in college, but she had had more of a family life in that respect than Declan had.

Taking care of his mother and providing temporary shelter for his niece wasn't the same thing as being a husband and a father, two things that Declan had never been.

In her opinion, he needed to live that life, experience those things. And that wouldn't happen with her. If she responded to him in any manner, chances were that she could be depriving him of enjoying that.

Damn, the more he looked at her, the more he found himself wanting to kiss her, Declan thought. There was something very heady—and now that he thought about it, stirring—about this woman. And it did bother him that she didn't seem to be responding to him in that way. After all, he wasn't exactly off-putting—if the way other women responded to him was any indication.

Just as Declan was about to give in to the very strong urge to kiss her, Midnight whinnied. The sound managed to break the spell weaving itself around him.

"I guess we'd better get back to the riding lesson," he told her.

Josie flashed a smile at him that he couldn't quite understand.

"I guess so," Josie agreed, relieved and yet somehow a tad disappointed as well.

On his feet, Declan extended a hand toward her, silently offering her help to get up.

She placed her hand in his and he closed his fingers around it. A very sharp tingle went through her, one she struggled to ignore. Josie let out a breath, not even realizing that she had been holding it until this second.

Taking a step back and putting a little distance between them, she felt steadier.

"We'd better get going," she said. "I know you have work to get to and I was hoping to get a few more pointers from you before I have to be getting back myself."

He nodded, taking Marigold's reins and holding the mare steady so that Josie could get on her.

It occurred to her that Declan was acting kinder toward her than he had the first time he had taken her for a riding lesson.

Maybe he was reacting to the fact that she had taken his niece off his hands a number of times already and he was being grateful for that.

Since silence was threatening to engulf them again, Declan made reference to his niece. "Shannon mentioned that in addition to working part-time at the animal shelter, you also help your brother and sister-in-law take care of their newborn twins."

"They're not exactly newborns anymore," Josie told him as they began the slow ride back. "They are going on seven months soon, but there's no arguing with the fact that they're certainly a handful." She smiled, thinking about her brother and his wife. "Of course, they had a rough start. They had to stay in the NICU for the first few months, which was very stressful on everyone. I just wanted to be able to be there—for the babies and for their parents," she told him.

"So you dropped everything and just came out to stay with them?" Declan questioned, filling in what he thought were things she had left out.

"There wasn't all that much to drop," Josie told her instructor. She didn't want him making a big deal out of what she was doing. "Like I mentioned the other day, my daughter is in college trying to do four years in three, so that keeps her very busy. I wouldn't be able to see her much, if at all.

"And I had my own catering business, so basically I was my own boss. I've been busy all my life and I like being useful, so coming out here to help my brother and his wife with their new family is as much for my sake as it is for theirs."

Declan shook his head. "I'm not all that sure I could do that in your place," he admitted.

"Sure you could. You are," she pointed out. "There are all sorts of ways of helping, you know." She could see that he looked unconvinced. "You took in your mother and your niece because they needed you."

Declan frowned, a furrow appearing between his brows. How had the conversation turned around like this? He wasn't looking for any sort of praise.

He shrugged. "Well, as for my mother," he told Josie, "I couldn't exactly turn my back on her."

"You'd be surprised how many sons and daughters could very easily do just that. And even if you took in your mother, that didn't mean you had to automatically take in your niece. I'm sure it probably wasn't exactly a package deal," she reminded him.

Recalling the situation, Declan laughed under his

breath. "Maybe not, but you don't know my mother. She wouldn't have given it a rest until I promised to take Shannon in. My mother used to do that when my father was alive, keep after him until he surrendered. And besides," he told her, "I'm not doing this alone. You're helping me with her," he reminded her.

"You couldn't have known that I'd offer to bring her to the animal shelter with me when you took the girl in. By the way," she added, "beneath that initial attitude, your niece is a really great kid."

He thought of his last confrontation with Shannon… but then thought about how things had been overall for the past week, with Shannon doing her chores, making conversation, showing real enthusiasm for the shelter. Things weren't perfect, but they sure were a lot better. "Well, the jury is still out on that," Declan told her.

She wasn't buying into his denial, but for now, she let him have it. "Take my word for it. She is."

He took a calculated guess what would make her say that. "Because she reminds you of your daughter?" Declan asked.

"No, because I've been watching her work with the animals," Josie contradicted. "Shannon's really great with them. She's got some pretty keen instincts when it comes to working with the new puppies."

"Like what?" he asked.

"Well, for one thing, Shannon has been socializing some of the puppies that were recently brought to the shelter." Turning toward Declan, she beamed, thinking of his niece. "She does amazing work with them.

"One of the puppies wouldn't even come out from

under this table where he had been hiding. When Shannon first started working with him, the poor thing was just whimpering and crying. Now he's playing with not just her but some of the other puppies as well. You should be very proud of Shannon," she told him. "Maybe you could come out sometime to observe her," she suggested suddenly.

Declan laughed shortly. "I really doubt she'd want me showing up at the shelter, looking over her shoulder and watching her."

She disagreed. "I think that you're wrong, Declan," she told him. "Every kid wants praise from the adult in their life."

He shrugged. "I figure you probably take care of that."

"If you mean praising her, I do," she willingly admitted. "But it's not the same thing. I'm not her uncle."

His brow wrinkled. "You're telling me she wants my approval?"

The man caught on quickly, she thought. "That's what I'm saying."

He easily dismissed that. "Well, I think you're wrong."

"Only one way to find out," she told him. "If I'm wrong, you've lost nothing. But if I'm right…" Her voice trailed off, allowing him to fill in the important part.

Declan shrugged, not about to commit himself. "We'll see," was all he told her.

The smile on her face was nothing short of encouraging. "I certainly hope so."

He felt as if he had just been given notice and pinned to the wall.

Chapter Eight

Normally, if his path crossed Shannon's, especially this early in the morning, Declan would just nod at his niece. But this morning, for some reason, Josie's words about Shannon wanting his approval had stuck in his head. So, against his better judgment, he initiated a conversation.

"You're up early," he said to the teenager, thinking that was a safe observation to make. He doubted that would get her back up, but then he never knew when it came to Shannon. Her attitude had been improving, but a display of temper could just be around the corner.

Surprised that her uncle had said anything at all to her, Shannon stopped walking. She felt if she didn't answer him, she could very well be rocking the boat.

She didn't want to take a chance on his grounding her. If he did, she knew that Josie wouldn't take her to the shelter.

"I had to get my chores out of the way first." She slanted a look at her uncle's face before going on. "Josie insists on it and she's coming to pick me up 'cause we're going to the animal shelter today."

"Oh." Declan would have been content to leave his reaction encased in the single word, but if he was going to test Josie's theory, he knew he would have to say more to Shannon than just one word. "This has turned into a regular thing, hasn't it? You going to the animal shelter," he added because Shannon was looking at him as if she wasn't sure exactly what he was getting at. "You like it? Helping out there?"

Somehow, his own words were sounding rather choppy and disjointed to him. He was about to restate his question when Shannon's expression shifted.

Declan wasn't prepared for the radiant smile that rose to his niece's lips.

"No," she answered. He thought she was being flippant, but then Shannon went on to tell him, "I love it."

He would have walked away, satisfied with that, but Declan knew he had left out the important, crucial test that went with this. Taking a deep breath, he forged ahead.

"Josie told me that you were doing a really great job with those dogs." He saw surprise and then pleasure wash over the girl's face. It encouraged him to push on. "She said that you were—how did she put it?—'socializing' them. Who taught you how to do that?" He was curious.

Shannon shrugged. "Nobody. I just felt like those dogs needed someone to love them and pay attention to them—like anyone else."

Declan couldn't help wondering if that was a less than subtle hint meant for him. About to make a comment, he paused and reconsidered the words that rose to his lips in response. Now that he thought about it, maybe he hadn't been all that supportive of his niece. When he had taken her in, he'd viewed her as one more responsibility when he already had too many to handle. What he hadn't done was think about her in terms of what she had to be feeling, being palmed off the way she had been on any available adult member of the family. First on his parents and now on him. Quite honestly, he hadn't thought about the situation from her point of view.

Maybe he should have, Declan told himself. It did seem rather bleak.

"You're probably right," he said. "Pretty sharp of you, figuring that out. I'm proud of you."

For his trouble, he was rewarded with a now all but blinding smile from Shannon.

And just like that, without even thinking about it, he had managed to bridge the gap that had existed between his niece and him. All because of Josie. Pretty damn sharp of the woman, he couldn't help thinking.

Just then there was a knock on the front door.

Shannon was instantly alert, coming to life even more than she already was.

"That's Josie," she announced happily, already heading toward the foyer.

"Wait," Declan said. When she turned to him, he told her, "I'll walk with you."

He half expected her to question why he wanted to do that and tell him to stay where he was, saying that she was perfectly capable of opening the door herself.

Instead, Shannon caught him off guard by saying, "Sure. C'mon."

So when the door opened, Josie found herself not only looking down at Shannon, but up at Declan, who was standing behind his niece.

If the sight of her tall, strapping instructor threw her, Josie didn't show it.

"Did I forget the part where you said you were coming along with us to the shelter?" Josie asked, cocking her head as she looked at Declan.

"No. I'm just accompanying Shannon to the front door—and after that I'm on my way out," he told her. And then he couldn't help adding, "Shannon was up early so she could do her chores before leaving with you."

Josie flashed a smile at the girl. "Nice to hear," she said, the remark aimed at both the girl and her uncle. And then she looked at Shannon. "So, are you ready to go to the shelter?"

"Oh, more than ready," the teen responded. Waving at her uncle, she fell into place beside her new best friend as they walked out the front door. "You know, Uncle D said you told him I was doing a good job," Shannon confided as if she was revealing a secret. "He actually said he was proud of me." The girl was fairly beaming again. "How about that?"

She was obviously thrilled by Declan's comment, Josie thought.

"Why wouldn't he be proud of you?" the woman asked. "You've come a long way in a really short amount of time," Josie pointed out. "You ask me, that's really something to be proud of," she said enthusiastically.

"Aw, it's no big deal," Shannon said, shrugging her shoulders.

"Don't sell yourself short, Shannon. It really *is* a big deal. Trust me," she went on as they got into her vehicle. "A lot of people wouldn't be able to do what you do with those dogs at the shelter. A lot of volunteers lose their patience—or they lose interest. You've stuck to it. If anything, you seem to become even more enthusiastic every time you come. I know that Bethany's really glad you volunteered."

Shannon looked a little confused. "Which one's Bethany?"

Josie found it amusing that the girl could keep all the puppies and grown dogs straight in her mind, but had trouble doing the same when it came to the people who ran the shelter.

"Bethany is the director at Furever Paws," Josie told her. Then, because she could see that her description didn't really ring any bells for Shannon, she added, "That's Meatball's mom," mentioning one of the dogs recently adopted from the shelter.

That caused the lightbulb to go off in Shannon's head. "Oh, her. She's the only one that Salty doesn't hiss at," the teen recalled.

Salty was the resident cat—the personal pet of the backyard breeder whose animals had been confiscated. "Salty doesn't hiss at you, either," Josie pointed out. The cat hissed at anyone who came close to him.

"That's because Salty ignores me," the teenager told her.

"Being ignored is still a lot better than being hissed at," Josie pointed out. "Don't worry, you'll win Salty over eventually," she promised just as she pulled her vehicle into the shelter parking lot.

She hadn't come to a full stop yet, but Shannon was already beginning to open up the door on her side to get out.

"Hey, slow down, Shannon. I don't want you getting hurt because you jumped out of my car before I could bring it to a full stop. The shelter will still be there half a minute from now," she promised.

With that, Josie pulled her car into a space that was close to the front of the shelter.

Hardly able to sit still, Shannon reminded Josie of a pot that was about to boil over. "Now?" Shannon asked hopefully.

Josie laughed. "Now."

And Shannon was out of the vehicle like a shot, hurrying to the shelter's front door. Josie only hoped that the teen would be lucky enough to find something that she was this excited about when she was finally able to go into the work world.

"Is Shannon gone already?" Ruth asked her son as she came out to turn her attention to preparing the lunch she was going to serve later.

"Shot out of the house like a bat out of hell," Declan told his mother. "But not before she finished doing her chores," he couldn't help marveling. "That woman is a miracle worker."

Ruth didn't have to ask what woman her son was referring to. "Maybe Josie learned that lavishing a little attention on a very lonely teenager yields a lot of dividends," she theorized.

"You and Dad used to take Shannon in every time Peggy decided to try to kick her drug habit," Declan remembered. "You can't tell me that Shannon didn't get that attention she needed from you."

"Actually, that was mostly your father's department. Those two had their own little mutual admiration society." Ruth smiled sadly as she remembered and went on working. "And besides, Shannon wasn't a teenager then." She shook her head. "Those adolescent hormones throw everything out of whack once they get going. Her grandfather is gone and Shannon's not staying in what she thought of as her second home." Ruth stopped working as she thought of the look on her granddaughter's face after she had been dropped off at Declan's ranch and her mother had pulled away in her car. "What used to be just being dropped off for a visit now seems like being abandoned."

Declan frowned. "Well, since you put it that way…" he said, his voice trailing off.

"I do, I don't get around like I used to. I can't do things with her the way I used to," Ruth answered, not very happy about the idea.

"But you're here, Mom," he pointed out. "Just not in the same location you used to be in."

"I might be here, Declan, but I'm not the person I used to be," she told her son sadly. "I was good at dealing with Shannon-the-little-girl, but I definitely wasn't any good at dealing with Shannon-the-teenager when she got here. I'm not proud of that."

Declan's mouth curved just a shade. "Then I suppose it's a lucky thing that Josie came to me for riding lessons when she did."

His mother smiled her agreement as she nodded. "Very lucky," she said. "It wouldn't hurt you to let that woman know how grateful you are that she's taken Shannon under her wing the way she has."

"Well, she didn't do it just out of the goodness of her heart," he reminded his mother, stealing a sliver of the pie she had taken out of the oven and was now cooling on the table. His mother slapped his hand away the way she used to do back when he was younger than Shannon was now. "After all, I am giving her free riding lessons, not to mention that the shelter probably welcomes having another volunteer to help out with the animals that they've taken in."

"Yes, yes, that's all true," Ruth agreed, nodding.

"But the bottom line, dear, is because of her, Shannon has stopped behaving like a wounded, sullen teenager." She looked at her son over her shoulder, her eyes meeting Declan's, warning him not to try to steal another sliver of pie.

But Declan was more interested in what his mother had to say than any piece of pie, good though that pie was.

"Where are you going with this?" he asked her, thinking it would save them both some time if he just asked outright.

"I was thinking that maybe we could invite Josie over for dinner to thank her. I could make something that she really likes to eat," Ruth suggested, her brown eyes gleaming with anticipation.

How did his mother know what Josie liked to eat? "Such as?" he asked.

Ruth smiled at her son, her manner indicating that he should have figured this out already. "Whatever she tells you that she likes."

The pieces were beginning to come together. "You want me to ask her?" he guessed, surprised and not a little uncomfortable at the idea.

"Well you're the one who's taking her out riding," his mother reminded him. "Ask her then."

"Mom, you're beginning to sound as if you've been watching too many of those reality TV shows," he complained.

"I am perfectly able to have an original thought of my own without taking a cue from one of those programs," she told her son. "In case you haven't noticed, I've been around longer than those programs have."

"I have no idea how long they've been around," he told his mother.

"Well, that makes two of us," his mother admitted with a careless shrug. The programs he had mentioned didn't interest her. Declan, Shannon and the woman who had come into their lives did.

Knowing how he could easily forget about things, Ruth reminded her son. "Just remember to ask Josie what her favorite food is when the two of you are out riding next, dear."

His mother made it sound as if their rides were for recreational purposes instead of part of his business. He decided it would do no good to point that fact out. His mother always viewed things exactly the way she wanted to.

He determined that it was best to approach her proposition logically. "And what sort of an excuse should I give her as to why I'm asking about her favorite food?" Declan wanted to know.

Ruth sighed. "Do I have to explain everything to you?" she asked. "Just tell that lovely woman that I wanted to thank her for all she's done for Shannon and my son by having her over for her favorite meal."

Red flags immediately went up. "Hold it. Back up," Declan ordered. "'To thank her for all she's done for *your son*?'" he questioned. "Aren't you going a little overboard here, Mom?"

His mother just smiled at him. "That's not the way I see it," she told him. And then, because she didn't feel like continuing the conversation along that line, she waved her son toward the door. "Don't you have some horses to work with today?" she asked.

"Yes, I do," he answered. "Thank God horses don't like to argue with me or give me grief," he told his mother.

"They also can't cook and clean for you," Ruth pointed out.

"Right now, Mom, that could only be a tradeoff," he replied. "See you later," he tossed over his shoulder as he left the house.

Getting into his Jeep, Declan drove over to the stables. Normally, he did enjoy working with the horses, but at the moment, his mother had planted that suggestion of dinner with Josie in his head and he couldn't seem to get rid of it or even move it to the back burner.

While the idea of approximating something like a date with Josie was certainly not a deal breaker— he could even view it as something refreshing—he didn't want his mother acting like some sort of an overzealous matchmaker. The very idea of having her try to create anything akin to a "date" was nothing short of pathetic.

He wouldn't have thought that it was actually possible, but his mother had managed to succeed in making him dread the next riding lesson he had scheduled with Josie.

Declan supposed that he wasn't under any obligation to do as his mother had suggested—but if he didn't, he knew the woman would keep harping on it until he finally gave in and asked Josie what her favorite meal was. Or worse, his mother would ask Josie directly what that meal was.

He supposed there was one good thing to come out of all this, he told himself as he walked into the stable. His mother was finally getting back to being her old self. It had been an exceptionally slow journey for her—and for him, since he was on the outside, observing her progress and worrying about her. Although by no means was she over the death of his father, she had begun to manage her pain and was now displaying interest in their family. That included both Shannon and him—and apparently, the woman who had entered all of their lives.

The woman, he thought now, who didn't seem to give him so much as a tumble.

Maybe having her over for dinner wasn't all that bad an idea after all, Declan mused. He decided to play it by ear when their next lesson came up.

Chapter Nine

Bunny and Birdie Whitaker, the affectionate nick-names for Josie's aunts Gwendolyn and Bernadette, had been the heart of the Furever Paws shelter ever since they'd founded it on land left to them by their parents. They'd run the shelter together for years, letting the animals in need and the larger animal-loving community fill their lives since neither woman had ever married.

But in the last few years, things started to change. Birdie, older than her sister by a year, became involved with a local veterinarian, Richard Jackson, referred to by one and all as Doc J. For the first time in her life, the relationship had Birdie shifting her priorities. While this was happening, Bunny, the young sister, had driven off in an RV with Stew Redmond, someone she had initially met on the internet and had been secretly communicating with for years.

It had seemed almost like a fairy-tale romance. Bunny had been engaged in her twenties, but after her fiancé died, she'd spent several decades alone. Everyone had been surprised but thrilled to see her ride off into the sunset. And certainly no one expected to see Bunny returning to Forest Springs anytime soon.

So when Josie spotted the battered RV pulling up in front of Grant's house early one morning, she was stunned and caught completely off guard.

As it happened, Josie was just passing the window that faced the front of the house when she saw the old RV pull up. Surprised, she stopped walking, curious to see who would wind up emerging.

To her, all motor homes looked more or less alike.

She definitely hadn't expected to see her aunt step out of the trailer when the door finally opened. She was even more surprised by the fact that her aunt appeared to be alone.

Thinking that she must have been mistaken, Josie stood there, waiting a minute to see if anyone else would come out of the RV, specifically the man her aunt had left town with, Stew Redmond.

But he didn't.

"Hey, Grant," she called out to her brother, who she knew was in the kitchen. "Did Aunt Bunny happen to call you or write to say that she was planning on coming home?"

"No," her brother answered. He crossed from the

kitchen over to Josie so he could look out the window to see whatever she was looking at. "If she sent any kind of a message, I didn't get it."

The next moment, Rebekah, holding Lucas in her arms, joined them.

"That *is* Aunt Bunny," she cried, surprised. "What do you think she's doing back? And where's that internet Don Juan she took off with?" Rebekah wondered out loud.

"It doesn't look like he's with her, as far as I can see," Grant observed.

"Maybe she dropped him off at the house. Birdie and Doc J are still living there, aren't they?" Josie asked Grant. It was hard keeping up with her aunts. The two women seemed to be leading far more active social lives than she currently was, Josie thought.

"They are," Rebekah confirmed. "But I'm not so sure that's what she did. Aunt Bunny doesn't look all that happy to me."

"Well, there's only one way to find out what's going on," Josie decided. The next moment, she was opening the front door. "Aunt Bunny, this is certainly a surprise," she declared, calling out to the woman as she stepped out of the house.

"For you and me both," Bunny admitted.

Grant and Rebekah exchanged looks. The couple appeared to be sharing the same thought. Their aunt's response did not sound very promising.

"What brings you back so soon?" Grant wanted to know. "When you left, you made it sound like you were off on this huge adventure for the next year or maybe even longer."

"Well, all adventures have to come to an end sometime," Bunny answered vaguely as she followed her nephew into the house.

"So Stew didn't come back with you?" Josie questioned, really hoping she was wrong. Her aunt had waited for so long to be in a relationship with a man. It would be awful if that relationship had fallen apart.

Bunny looked far from happy. "Doesn't look that way, does it?"

As far as Josie was concerned, that was a nonanswer. However she strongly suspected that, for some reason, her aunt was alone again. "Is there anything we can do?" Josie asked.

"Yes, you can stop asking questions," Bunny told her niece uncharacteristically sharply. The woman frowned. "I'd rather not talk about it right now."

Grant nodded. "Okay, sure," he agreed. "We didn't mean to sound like we're prying. We just all care about you, Aunt Bunny."

The woman pulled herself together. "I appreciate that," she replied.

"Are you staying at your house?" Rebekah wanted to know, switching to what she viewed as a safer topic. "Because you're more than welcome to—"

"Stay here?" Bunny guessed. "Thank you, but unless I'm planning on curling up in the fireplace, I'd say you have a full house at the moment," she said, nodding toward Josie. And then she looked at the baby in Rebekah's arms. "Who's this lovely little girl?" she asked, running her hand along the baby's downy hair.

"That 'little girl' is Lucas," Grant corrected his aunt tactfully.

"This is the boy?" Bunny asked, moving in for a closer look. "Sorry," she apologized.

"Nothing to be sorry about. At this age, unless I'm changing them, I still tend to get them mixed up," Rebekah said.

"So, are you back for good, Aunt Bunny?" Josie asked, then realized that from the expression on her aunt's face, she would have been better off keeping the question to herself.

"Certainly looks that way now, doesn't it?" Bunny asked, refusing to give her niece any sort of an actual answer. It was all too fresh and painful for her at the moment.

Josie pressed her lips together, but then decided to speak again. Since she had already put her foot in her mouth, Josie felt that she had nothing to lose if she said anything further. And maybe, although she wouldn't admit it, Bunny could use some positive words. So Josie went ahead.

"Well, things have a way of changing," she told her aunt.

Bunny made an inexplicable noise. "I think I've had just about enough change for now." There was a note of sad finality in her voice.

Ever mindful of what Grant's aunt had to be going through, Rebekah decided to switch gears. "Can I get you something to eat, or perhaps some coffee to drink?" she offered.

"No, that's all right. I'm fine, I stopped at Veniero's on my way here," Bunny told her nephew's wife.

"But isn't Veniero's closed at this hour?" Grant asked.

As far as he knew, the popular Italian restaurant had only recently begun to open its doors for lunch. When it was first opened, the restaurant was intended to be an elegant and romantic alternative to some of the more casual spots in town. A high-end, sophisticated establishment—with a price tag to match.

"It was," Bunny agreed, "but I got them to open up for me." It wasn't a boast, it was just a simple fact. Everyone loved Bunny—she'd probably talked half the town into adopting or fostering pets at one point or another. She was a surrogate aunt to just about everyone who had ever met her. And that meant she was not the kind of person people were comfortable saying no to.

In response, Grant could only smile. That sounded just like his aunt.

"Of course you did." Just then, another lusty voice could be heard wailing from the nursery. "Maybe you'd like to meet the other newest addition to the Whitaker clan?" Grant offered. "Lily is even louder than her twin brother."

The rather somber expression on Bunny's face receded. The woman smiled and nodded. Bunny thought of babies as a welcome diversion. She knew that they could get her mind off her current situation, if only for a little while.

"I'd love to," Bunny told her nephew.

"What do you think made her come back without her traveling companion? She seemed so gung-ho when they first took off," Rebekah said, turning toward her sister-in-law after her husband had led his aunt to the nursery.

Josie shook her head. "When it comes to Aunt Bunny, you just never know. Possibly her mystery suitor didn't turn out to be the man she was expecting him to be. Or maybe, conversely, Aunt Bunny and her beau just spent too much time together and wound up getting on each other's nerves. That kind of thing happens a lot," she speculated. "In that case, maybe Aunt Bunny came back here in order to get some much needed time apart from her 'gentleman caller.'"

Rebekah looked out the window at the trailer that was now parked in front of her beloved house. "You know, you might have something there. That RV she was driving doesn't look as if it exactly has that much room for two traveling companions who ever want some space to themselves."

Josie nodded in agreement. "Not unless you're talking about those travelers being two hamsters."

The comment made Rebekah laugh, really laugh, as she pictured two hamsters rattling around in the RV. She laughed so hard that tears came to her eyes. Rebekah wiped away one tear that had rolled down her cheek.

"Thanks," Rebekah told her sister-in-law. "I really needed that."

"Any time," Josie told her cheerfully. "That's what I'm here for." And then she moved in closer to Rebekah, looking at the baby in her arms. "Now why don't you let me take him from you?" she suggested, nodding at Lucas. "Go socialize, talk to Aunt Bunny. If I don't miss my guess, I think that Aunt Bunny really needs to have her family around her right about now."

"But she said she didn't want to talk," Rebekah protested.

"That's okay," Josie told her sister-in-law. "Aunt Bunny doesn't have to talk. Just knowing that her family is there for her and cares about her is enough for now. She'll talk when she's ready to."

Nodding her head, Rebekah quickly left the room.

Because of her aunt's unexpected return to Forest Springs, Josie decided to cancel both her riding lesson and her planned trip to the rescue shelter for that day. She felt that she would be far more needed just hanging around at Grant's house.

As it turned out, her aunt wound up putting off returning to the family home where she had grown up with her siblings. Josie got the definite impression that Bunny didn't want to deal with Birdie's questions about her unexpected return.

Since both sisters were stubborn in their own way, Josie knew that wasn't a confrontation either of the sisters would welcome.

She would have thought that Declan would have welcomed the lesson cancellation. She was surprised when she heard him ask why she wasn't coming. At least that was an easy enough question to answer.

"My aunt Bunny suddenly turned up," she explained. "I sensed that she definitely wasn't happy about coming back sooner than she'd expected, so I thought I'd stay and try to smooth out any rough patches that might come up for Grant and Rebekah," she told Declan. "Would you mind if I rescheduled?"

"Sure. Just pick a day and I'll see if I need to move some things around," he told her.

That really surprised her. Josie had fully expected the instructor to just dismiss her, saying something to the effect that he'd see if he was free, not that he would see what he had to move around to accommodate the rescheduled lesson.

Would wonders never cease? she couldn't help thinking.

"Thank you," Josie responded. "Oh, and would you tell Shannon that I won't be able to bring her to the shelter with me this afternoon?"

"Why not?" he wanted to know.

That made two unexpected responses in less than a few minutes, she thought. "Because I'm not going to the shelter today. Aunt Bunny can come on rather strong, not to mention that she's obviously dealing with something and could very well use a shoulder to lean on."

"How did you wind up handling the world's problems?" he asked, curious.

She didn't know if he was making fun of her or if he was asking a legitimate question. In either case, she just answered him as if it was a serious question.

"Just something that seemed to have happened along the way," she told him. And then she stressed, "Don't forget to tell Shannon I'm sorry I won't be taking her and that I promise I'll make it up to her."

Before he could make any comment on that, Declan realized the woman he was talking to had terminated the phone call.

He closed his phone. Well, it looked as if he wasn't going to be asking Josie about her favorite meal today, he thought philosophically.

Chapter Ten

Josie was finally able to get away for her next horse-back riding lesson, not when she planned, but a few days later.

When she walked into the stable that afternoon, she was surprised to hear muffled sobs coming from one of the stalls. Knowing the sound couldn't possibly be coming from a horse, Josie made her way over toward the source of the incredibly unhappy sound.

That was when she found Shannon huddled in a stall. The teen was sobbing her heart out.

Declan's niece didn't even seem to be aware that she was even there, Josie thought.

Sinking down next to the girl, Josie slipped her arm around the teenager's shaking shoulders. "Shannon, honey, what happened?" Josie asked.

Shannon sounded as if her heart was breaking.

The girl's eyes were red-rimmed when she looked up at Josie. It took several seconds before she was finally able to get her words out. "There's a bake sale at school tomorrow," Shannon sobbed.

Josie was well aware that Shannon was desperately trying to fit in at this new high school that Declan had finally registered her for, but she had no idea how this bake sale could be such an incredible source of distress for the girl.

"And that's a problem because?" Josie asked the teen, not certain why a bake sale would make her cry like this.

More tears spilled down Shannon's cheeks. "Because I don't know how to bake and Grandma's arthritis flared up. Her hands hurt too much for her to be able to cook *or* bake anything."

Declan walked into the stable just then and he was able to shed more light on the situation.

"I offered to pick up some cupcakes from the grocery store, but Shannon told me that that store-bought isn't good enough."

Shannon turned her tear-stained, red face toward Josie. It was difficult for her to speak. "According to the rules, whatever I bring to the sale has to be homemade," she cried. "That means I have to make it. I can't bake, Josie. I'll be the only one not bringing anything." She hiccupped as another sob followed her declaration.

"No, you won't," Josie told her firmly. "C'mon,

honey," she urged. "Get on your feet. You and I have work to do."

Shannon blinked, not sure if she was hearing her friend correctly. "We do?" she questioned.

"Yes, we do. I need you to 'assist' me," Josie told the teenager. She held out a tissue to the girl, waiting to help her up.

Shannon closed her hand around the tissue. She looked at Josie uncertainly. It hadn't occurred to her to ask the woman for help.

"You know how to bake?" she asked Josie.

"I'd better," Josie laughed softly. "I ran my own catering business before I came out here."

Shannon's eyes widened. She could hardly believe her luck. "Really?"

Josie lifted the girl's head, tilting it back with the crook of her index finger. "Have I ever lied to you?" she asked the teen.

"Not that I know of," Shannon answered, looking at Josie cautiously.

No question about it. The girl was definitely her uncle's niece, Josie thought.

"Well, I haven't," she told Shannon with a note of finality. "I was baking before I was ten years old." Then, taking in a deep breath, Josie said, "If this sale is taking place tomorrow, we need to get started."

The teenager saw a conflict forming. "But what about your riding lesson?" Shannon asked, looking over her shoulder at her uncle. He hadn't said anything about Josie volunteering to help her. She knew he didn't like his plans suddenly changing on him.

Thinking that the girl felt bad about her having to miss her lesson, Josie merely shrugged. "Don't worry about it. If I can miss a lesson because my aunt Bunny needed me, I can certainly miss a riding lesson because you need me. The way I see it," Josie went on, "this counts as an emergency."

She was rewarded with Shannon's radiant smile. But even so, despite the rebellious noises she had initially made when she had come to live at the farmhouse, the teen looked toward her uncle for permission.

"So it's okay?" she asked Declan.

"Hey, Josie told you that she wanted to help you. Who am I to get in the way of that?" he asked his niece.

Josie looked at Shannon's uncle, pleased with his response. She knew she was pushing her luck with this next statement.

"You might have to go to the store for us," Josie told him. "You probably don't have everything that we're going to need for this project."

Declan looked at the woman his niece now thought of as her new patron saint. "Just how much are you planning on baking?" he needed to know.

Josie in turn looked at Shannon. "A lot," she responded.

With that, she walked into Declan's kitchen and began rolling up her sleeves.

Ruth was sitting at the table, having a cup of tea. Surprised at their entrance, she set down her cup.

"What's going on?" Declan's mother asked as she looked from Josie to her granddaughter.

"Josie's going to help me with the bake sale," the teen happily announced, beaming. "Isn't that great, Grandma?"

Ruth had been feeling terrible all morning because she wasn't able to help her granddaughter. Hearing that Josie was stepping in to help out was the perfect solution to the problem.

"Bless you, dear," she told the younger woman with feeling.

"Josie said she had her own catering company back in—where did you say you were from?" Shannon asked the woman who had come to her rescue.

"Florida," Josie answered. Walking over to the pantry, she opened the double doors and looked over the shelves. "I was right," she said to Declan, making a quick inventory. "I'm going to need you to take a quick ride over to the grocery store. Just let me make up a list," she told him.

Finding a pad, Josie pulled it over and quickly began writing things down as they occurred to her.

When she was done, she held the sheet of paper out to Declan.

"You sure you need all this stuff?" Declan questioned, his eyes moving quickly over the page. "This looks like an awfully lot of ingredients for a school bake sale."

"Better to have too much than to run out right in the middle," she told him. "Besides, none of this will go to waste. I can always come back and make some more baked goods if you find you come down with a sudden craving."

The comment brought a smile to Ruth's lips as she glanced over toward her son. Her smile seemed to fairly shout "I told you so."

Declan was not about to argue with his mother at this point. Especially not in front of Josie. Or Shannon, who was clearly listening intently. Taking the sheet of paper from Josie, he glanced at the list again. He folded the paper several times over then shoved the resulting tiny square into the pocket of his jeans.

"Not sure where I'm going to find all these things," he warned Josie and his niece. This sort of thing took him way out of his element.

"All those things can usually be found in the same aisle in the store," Josie told Declan. "Grocery clerks like to make things easy for their customers," she assured him. "And if you have any doubts, just ask," Josie said.

Declan frowned. He wasn't holding out too much hope about the grocery store excursion at the moment. He had never liked going shopping, putting it off to the last minute if not even longer. To him, grocery shopping was something to be endured and came in just a little above doing hard penance.

When his mother had come to live with him, that had become her department. But only when her arthritis wasn't acting up. At the moment, that wasn't the case.

"Easy. Right," he commented under his breath just before he went out the door.

* * *

It amazed Declan, when he returned with all the groceries and Josie got started, to see the woman he was teaching how to ride showing him another side of herself.

He was used to simple dishes, not to the kind of things that appeared to require this amount of effort to create.

As he watched, Josie proceeded to bake up a storm. Several hours went by, but by the time she and her new "assistant" were finally finished working together, "they" had produced a large tray of mint chocolate-chip brownies, several dozen beautifully decorated sugar cookies, plus a monumentally large tray of chocolate biscotti.

The combined tempting aroma wafting from the baked goods was almost too irresistible for him to resist.

Declan looked around his kitchen. It seemed as if every single inch of space was covered with the end result of her labors.

Declan looked at the various pastries. He had never thought of himself as having a sweet tooth—until now. He could almost feel himself salivating.

"You know, this is almost too tempting to ignore," he told his niece.

Shannon didn't know if she should be worried or if he was joking. She had never found herself in this sort of a situation with her uncle before. With the advent of Josie in their lives, everything seemed to have gotten more comfortable. But she hoped that didn't mean that her uncle would start eating the product of her hard work.

"Well, you'd better ignore it," Shannon told her uncle. "I need to bring everything that's here in to the bake sale," she said then pleaded, "Please promise me you don't eat any of it."

"Not even one piece?" he asked his niece.

He was serious, Shannon thought. "Josie." The teen all but wailed nervously, asking her mentor for help.

"He's just teasing you, honey," Josie told the girl. "If he wants to eat any of these things—" she waved her hand at all the items that were left cooling on the table "—he's going to have to come down to the school and buy it like everyone else."

Declan laughed dismissively. "It's not like I have all this extra time on my hands," he pointed out.

She realized that her solution had brought up another problem for Declan. "All right," she said, picking up the apron she had just removed. Putting it back on, she tied the ends together again, forming a bow. "Then I'll bake something just for you."

Declan was about to tell her not to go to all that trouble, but he had to admit that the smell of the baked goods was really beginning to get to him. He was truly tempted.

Still, he finally forced himself to say, "You don't have to do that."

She knew when she was on the receiving end of a halfhearted protest. "Oh, I think I do," she told him.

"Do you want to sit here and keep me company, or just come back for the finished product?"

He was somewhat tempted by the former, but there were still things he had to get to. The ranch didn't just run itself, no matter how much, at times, he wished that it could.

"I'll be back as soon as I can," Declan promised Josie.

"And I'll probably still be here," she answered.

It was the "probably" that got to him and made Declan hurry. As it was, he managed to return just before dinnertime.

But when he walked in, he found that Josie had already left.

"She didn't stay?" he asked his mother, trying not to sound as disappointed as he felt.

"No," his mother answered. "The poor dear was worn to a frazzle," Ruth told her son. "She had spent all that time baking those things for Shannon's bake sale, then," she added significantly, "a bunch of baked goods just for you. When she was finished, she also saw the way I was holding that whisk as I was trying to make mashed potatoes. She insisted that I sit down and take it easy while *she* went on to make dinner." She smiled broadly. "I tell you, Declan, that girl is one in a million. Maybe even two million," she declared.

Declan rolled his mother's words over in his mind then said, "Well, you won't get an argument out of me. What did she wind up making?" he asked, referring to the aroma he smelled coming from the oven.

"Dinner," his mother answered simply. When he looked at the woman quizzically, she told him, "If you can't figure it out, then my guess is that your sense of smell died of boredom after that bland slop you've been cooking for all these years."

Declan took in another breath, deeper this time. It smelled wonderful, he realized. "It's fried chicken, isn't it?"

"Right on the first try, dear. Maybe your sense of smell isn't dead," she told her son, smiling at him. "So, are you just going to sit there, sniffing, or are you going to bring the chicken over to the table and do it justice?" she wanted to know.

"Guess I'll do it justice," Declan said, picking up the platter and bringing it over.

Placing a piece on his plate, he heard a side door close. The next moment, Shannon entered the room.

"Hey, you weren't going to eat without me, were you?" the teen wanted to know. She slid into a chair at the dinner table.

Declan quirked a brow. "Where were you?" he asked.

"I was just putting away the goodies that Josie made for the bake sale," she told her uncle.

Declan had his own ideas about that. "You could have left them out. It's not like the things she made were going to spoil before tomorrow," he told her.

"No," Shannon agreed. "But they could very well have gotten eaten."

"Are you saying that you thought I'd eat them all on you?" Declan asked, feigning surprise.

"Not even your uncle has *that* big an appetite," Ruth told her granddaughter as she came to Declan's defense.

Shannon looked a little skeptical.

"There's always a first time," she told her grandmother. "And those things that Josie made all smelled really delicious." She smiled happily. "They'll probably all sell out within the first half hour," she predicted. "Hey—" she suddenly had a thought as she helped herself to some of the fried chicken "—do you think that Josie could teach me how to make at least some of those baked goodies?" she asked her grandmother.

"I don't see why not," Ruth answered. "She's a nice lady who's obviously very generous with her time." The words were meant for her granddaughter but she was looking at Declan as she said them. "Do you think that fried chicken is her favorite meal?" she asked her son. Unconsciously, she was stretching her hand, trying to get feeling and mobility back in it.

He thought it over. "Well, that all depends," he answered.

She wasn't sure where he was going with this. "On what?"

"On whether or not this was the only thing you had on hand for her to make for dinner," he told his mother.

Because she didn't trust her memory the way she used to, Ruth walked over to the refrigerator. Opening the door, she looked inside.

The shelves were very close to being empty. She

remembered that she'd meant to go shopping and then her arthritis had kicked in, making going to the store for food a real challenge.

"Looks like the chicken was it," she told her son. "But Josie certainly did a good job of making it."

"I didn't say she didn't," Declan answered. "All I said was that she didn't have another choice when it came to making dinner, so maybe fried chicken isn't her favorite meal."

Ruther frowned at her son. "You're just saying that because you don't want to invite her over."

"No, I'm just saying that because I honestly don't know if it's her favorite meal. But you can still make fried chicken. As I remember it, you make one mean fried chicken."

Ruth smiled, massaging her hands as she tried to get the sharp pain she felt in them to recede. Despite the fact that the pain had settled in, she offered her son a pleased smile.

"I do, don't I?" she asked brightly.

Bringing his plate over to the sink, he paused, leaning over to kiss his mother's forehead. "You really do," he assured her with conviction.

Chapter Eleven

Because it was a nice spring day, Shannon's high school bake sale was held outdoors. That meant that it was open to the general public, allowing at least half of the residents of Spring Forest to drop by the sale at one point or other. A good many of those residents showed up to support either their own student who was attending the high school, or the students in general.

Shannon discovered that one such parent was also the owner of the local coffee shop. Surveying all the tables displaying the baked goods that had been brought in, that coffee shop owner stopped by Shannon's table. She was obviously intrigued by all the baked goods Shannon had brought but she seemed especially interested in the chocolate biscotti.

The woman seemed to linger at the display for several minutes before she looked up at Shannon and finally asked the girl, "Do those chocolate biscottis taste as good as they look?"

"They taste even better," Shannon assured the woman confidently.

Just before leaving her the day before, Josie had given the teen a few tips when it came to selling the baked goods.

"Remember," she had said, "you have to believe in your product. If you don't, no one else will. Those people attending the bake sale certainly won't spend their hard-earned money on your baked goods if something else catches their eye. So if a potential buyer wants to know if what you're selling tastes good," Josie had added, gathering her things together, "just smile mysteriously at them and say something to the effect that they'll just have to try the cookie, or cupcake, or biscotti and judge for themselves."

"Is that how you did it with your catering business?" Shannon had asked her, trying to absorb as much as she could from her mentor.

"Usually when they came to me, they were already sold because one of their friends recommended me to them," Josie'd explained. "But if they just came to me at random, then yes, that's what I would say to them." Ready to leave, Josie had patted the teen's shoulder. "Good luck, Shannon. You're going to do fine," she'd promised.

The woman who had just asked Shannon about the biscotti decided that they looked too good for her to pass up. Taking out her wallet, she bought one, then sampled it right there on the spot.

Her expression indicated that she had expected the pastry to be good, but not *this* good. Eating the biscotti, it seemed as if her whole mouth was smiling.

"Did you have help with these?" she asked the teen.

"Yes, ma'am. The lady taking riding lessons from my uncle Declan helped me," Shannon answered. "She said she had a catering company back in Florida."

Without meaning to, the woman wound up consuming the entire biscotti right on the spot. She purchased another one. Handing over money for the second biscotti, the woman made a request of the teen. "Could you ask this lady who worked with you to create these wonderful biscottis if she would be interested in selling them to my shop on a regular basis? I can definitely handle as many as she can make," the woman promised.

The smile Shannon flashed at the woman went from ear to ear. This was turning out to be far better than she had hoped.

"I will definitely ask her that," Shannon promised.

To ensure that the message would be delivered, the woman handed Shannon a business card that advertised her coffee shop. "Don't forget," she requested.

Shannon tucked away the woman's card. "Oh, I won't," she vowed. She liked the idea of giving Shannon an additional reason to remain in town.

After the coffee shop owner left, there seemed to be an endless line of people approaching Shannon's table to buy the items she had on display.

Although Declan had told his niece that he didn't have the time to stop in at the school's bake sale, he knew how much doing well at this sale meant to her. He decided that even though he was busy, he needed to stop by to see how things were going for Shannon. If the baked goods that Josie had helped her make didn't seem to be selling, he was prepared to purchase at least a few of them to show his support.

Part of Declan was afraid that his stoic niece might even need comforting if the sale wasn't going as well as she had hoped.

But when he stopped by the high school's sale, he found that there didn't appear to be any goods left on her table. He was pleased and relieved to see that Shannon was all sold out.

"Looks like I didn't have to worry about you," Declan told his niece. He marveled as he looked at the empty table again. "You did good, kid."

Shannon spread her hands out at the empty table in front of her, hardly able to believe it herself. "I sold *everything*," she cried happily. "Isn't that great?" she squealed. "Even Mrs. Winters, the principal, came by to congratulate me. I told her that I couldn't take all of the credit. I said that Josie helped me."

"Oh, she 'helped' you, did she?" Declan repeated, amused.

"Okay, I helped her," Shannon conceded then told

her uncle, "Josie said I could keep that a secret if I wanted to. But I guess it's not right. I should give her all the credit." She beamed at him, saying, "I'm really glad that you started giving her those riding lessons, Uncle D."

He really couldn't get over the change in his niece. He had never seen her quite like this before. It was like night and day between the teenager who had first walked into his house and the one he found himself talking to right now.

"Well, if she can make you smile like that, Shannon, then so am I," he told her.

Declan saw no point in telling his niece that the woman intrigued him as well. Not until something came of that situation at any rate. He might have loosened up a little, at least to a degree, but he still wasn't very big on sharing his personal details.

Because of his work schedule, the only free time Declan could manage to come up with was in the morning, right after Shannon left for school. So that was when he arranged with Josie to come over so she could take her missed riding lesson.

When Josie arrived at the stables, the first thing out of her mouth was to ask about Shannon.

"So how did the bake sale wind up going?" she wanted to know.

"Shannon didn't stop smiling all day. At least, every time that I saw her, she was positively glowing. She managed to sell everything she had brought down to the last crumb." Declan looked at the woman as they rode out of the stable. "I know that I've got you to thank for that." He paused then said, "Thank you."

"Your niece is a good kid," Josie assured him. "I just baked some things that she could bring in for that sale. Shannon was simply really trying to fit in and she was afraid that she wouldn't. I wanted to make sure that she had something to bring, but if I hadn't been around, it would have all worked out anyway."

Declan wasn't as convinced as she was and he said as much. "I don't know about that. Kids that age are pretty aware of their shortcomings. They tend to magnify what they do wrong and downplay whatever they get right—that is, if they don't have a huge ego," he qualified.

Josie looked at him, surprised. "That's pretty insightful for a bachelor," she told him. He had the potential of being a really good father when the time came, she couldn't help thinking.

"Yeah, well she doesn't always make it easy, but I do care about her," Declan confided. "Poor kid already feels like her mother keeps abandoning her, doing that with a fair amount of regularity. Couldn't make her feel like she couldn't depend on me as well. It just wouldn't be right," he pointed out. "As for you," he went on to tell Josie, smiling at the woman, "you're the big hero in her book."

His observation made Josie laugh out loud.

The sound wove its way deep into his system. He liked how it seemed to cast sunshine all through him. "What's so funny?" he asked after a beat.

Josie's eyes were twinkling as she answered. "I

knew making mint chocolate-chip brownies would come in handy someday."

"It certainly did," he agreed, smiling.

They had come to a stream on his property. Reaching it, Declan pulled up his stallion's reins. "Why don't we stop here?" he suggested. "The horses could use the break. And the water," he noted. "The day's already getting warm and it isn't even noon."

She saw no reason not to agree. Pulling up on Marigold's reins, Josie brought the mare to a halt right next to his stallion. Once she was certain that her horse had stopped moving, she dismounted.

Declan took the time to observe her form and then he nodded, more to himself than at her. "You're getting better at that," he told her.

The casual comment pleased her. Coming from him, it seemed like high praise. "Thank you." She patted the mare's neck. "I think that Marigold's getting used to me."

"There is that," he agreed, his mouth curving ever so slightly. "But you're also becoming more confident and the mare can pick up on that," Declan told her.

"I guess we're learning about each other," she concluded, pleased that she was making some sort of headway and that Declan had actually noticed it.

Not wanting to make any further comment about herself, Josie looked around. "This is really very pretty country," she told Declan.

He glanced around ever so slowly, as if he really hadn't assessed the area before.

"Yes, it is," Declan agreed. "I'm usually working too hard at any given time to actually notice that," he admitted.

She turned toward him. "Maybe you should do what people are always saying to do. Every once in a while, you should stop and just smell the roses." She knew that had to sound so trite, but she really did believe in what she was saying.

Declan looked at her, about to make a comment about her less than original observation, but the words seemed to just stick in his mouth.

Damn but she looked pretty, he thought.

More than pretty, he silently amended. With the sunlight threading through her hair, highlighting it until it seemed to almost to shimmer like strands of gold begging to be touched, she looked absolutely gorgeous. He could almost feel that softness beneath his fingertips.

"Maybe I should," he murmured, although smelling roses was the furthest thing from his mind.

His voice almost seemed to caress her.

Josie told herself that she was imagining things. That Declan was just making conversation and that she was allowing her imagination to run away with her. But being logical didn't seem to be helping.

She felt a warmth spreading all through her, touching every part of her body like rays of sunshine.

Josie could feel her very skin growing hot, and the weather had nothing to do with it.

And then, before she could think of some sort of a response to make in answer to what Declan had just said, she felt the man gently thread his fingers through her hair, drawing her face up closer to his.

He lowered his head until his mouth was barely a breath away from hers. Josie could actually *feel* his breath slipping along her skin.

Her heart started racing.

This was where she drew the line, she told herself. This was where she pulled back, curtailing this moment before it could blossom into something more, into what she was secretly hoping would happen.

And yet...

And yet who was she kidding? No matter how hard she tried, Josie couldn't make herself draw away, couldn't even make herself create so much as a sliver of distance between them.

In fact, she caught herself *willing* the moment to happen.

Her heart was really racing now. Any second, she was certain it was going to wind up leaping out of her chest.

Declan was looking into her eyes, searching for some sign that he had presumed too much, that she actually wanted him to pull away and give her some breathing space so that she could retreat from this mistake they were both about to make.

He was finding himself getting lost in her incredibly blue eyes, aware just how damn hard it would be for him if he did have to pull away. Even so, Declan knew that he *would* pull away if she told him to because there was no way he wanted to just force himself on Josie in any manner, shape or form.

But the only thing he saw in her eyes was blatant hunger.

Hunger that matched the hunger he felt growing in his own soul.

Tilting her head back just the slightest bit, Declan finally lowered his mouth and brought his lips down over hers.

The burst of energy, of blazing fulfillment, he felt rocked him down to the very toes of his boots. He was suddenly made a prisoner of the sensation that was shooting through his body, holding him so very tightly in its grip.

Without even thinking about it, he closed his arms around Josie, held her fast against him and lost himself in the very warmth, the heated glow, of her. The sensation completely wrapped itself all around him.

For the very first time in his life, he felt himself becoming a part of someone else, especially when she wrapped her arms around him and stood on her toes so that she was able to sink into his kiss more fully.

This is insane, a voice in her head echoed.

All the reasons she had already laid out in her mind why this was a bad thing came rushing back to her in bright, vivid detail. She had decided she was just too old for this man.

Nothing had changed since then.

Well, maybe one thing had changed. The deep, all-consuming hunger for him had only managed to become even more intense. As he went on kissing her, his lips feeling as if they were invading every part of her without moving an inch, that hunger within her only grew stronger.

Even though she knew this was wrong, even though she knew she would regret this move, Josie still couldn't make herself stop, couldn't make herself draw back much less pull away.

Whatever regrets she would have would come later. As for now, all she wanted to do was sink even more deeply into his kiss.

Nothing else seemed to matter.

Damn but he wanted her. Wanted to take her, to make love with her. And yet he knew that whatever pleasure he would derive from making that moment become a reality, he would eventually wind up paying for it.

Dearly.

This wasn't like him, Declan chastised himself. It was as if a spell had been cast over him.

For all he knew, she might even terminate any contact between them. And in his heart, he knew that also would include his niece. Shannon would never forgive him for that. Since she had just shown him that there was this happy new side to her, he couldn't allow his own needs to cause that side to just disappear. That would be beyond cruel.

So, though it took almost superhuman effort on his part, Declan forced himself to stop. Stop kissing her, if not stop wanting her, since he doubted that the latter was even possible.

Taking a breath to fortify himself, Declan drew back. When he saw the confused, partially wounded look in Josie's eyes, he almost caved. But somehow he managed to hold his ground.

It was far from easy.

"We're going too fast," Declan told her, holding her face in his hands and creating a sliver of distance between them.

Her heart was still slamming wildly against her chest. It was extremely hard for her to pull herself together, but she knew that Declan was right. Knew that if he pushed the situation even just the tiniest bit, she would more than willingly make love with him.

And that, she was very certain, would cause both of them to draw away afterward. Once that happened, most likely they would wind up never seeing one another again.

She drew in a shaky breath. She couldn't allow her own personal hunger to torpedo everything else that had been created, like her friendship with a lonely teenager.

Josie's mouth curved ever so slightly as she nodded, silently agreeing with him.

"You're right," she told Declan, her voice barely above a whisper. "We almost let something happen that would have changed everything."

Turning away, she mounted her mare. "I think we need to be getting back."

He didn't want to be getting back. He wanted to remain here. With her. But he knew he had to agree. It was the only way to keep himself from caving in.

He was too smart to just live in the moment without being aware of the repercussions that would have.

"Yeah, we do," he replied, getting back up on Midnight.

As they rode to the stable, it was mostly in silence.

Chapter Twelve

Josie tried not to think about what had very nearly happened at the lake the day before. Instead, she forced herself to focus on the rest of her life in Spring Forest.

Taking everything else except what had gone down between Declan and her into consideration, this was what she had going on in North Carolina: helping with her brother's twins, working at the animal shelter and doing a lot of baking that she distributed around town.

Well, all of that plus worrying about her daughter, but she could do that from anywhere. Although they texted frequently and talked on the phone every week or two, it had been a long time since she'd seen Hannah in person. And the fact that her daughter wasn't coming home this summer or, most likely, the following summer as well, meant that the situation with Hannah wasn't really a deciding factor in where Josie ended up. Hannah was so driven to get her medical degree as quickly as possible that she kept going with classes even during summer semesters. Because of that, there really was no reason for her to go back to Florida at all.

If she wanted more to keep her occupied, her catering business could easily be restarted anywhere— like here. Shannon had given her the business card she had gotten from the woman who ran the coffee shop. When Josie had called the woman to thank her for the compliments she had relayed to Shannon, the coffee shop owner made it clear that those were not just empty words. She had really enjoyed the biscottis and she was very serious about selling the chocolate baked goods in her shop.

"You bake them and I'll sell them" were the woman's exact parting words.

Josie felt more needed here in Spring Forest than she had in the last year she had spent in Florida. Both her mother and her sister were busy running their business, so they didn't need her on the premises.

As for Declan...well, what had happened between them yesterday hadn't exactly been a deal breaker, she thought now with a smile. That little episode actually came under the heading of "we'll see."

Yes, Josie admitted, she was older than the horse breeder, but then she wasn't looking for marriage or anything even remotely like that. Realistically, a little companionship right about now wasn't all that bad an idea, Josie realized.

And even that might not actually happen, she told herself. Declan had kissed her and she had kissed him back. That didn't exactly constitute an earth-shaking event or the start of an ongoing relationship. For all she knew, this "we'll see thing" between them could very well go nowhere. It certainly wasn't a reason for her not to consider relocating permanently to Spring Forest.

However, the possibility that arose from that encounter was definitely an idea, she told herself, to keep on the front burner.

For now, she would continue doing what needed to be done. That included helping out at the shelter, which also meant bringing Shannon with her whenever the girl was available and *wanted* to come.

Under that same heading she included not just helping out with the twins, but gathering as much useful information as she could find that might help Grant and Rebekah to capably raise the twins.

From where she stood, she and her brother and sister-in-law could stand to avail themselves of as much information as was out there.

So when Bethany, the newly appointed director of the animal shelter, had suggested that she accompany Bethany to one of the Working Parents get-togethers that was being held, Josie agreed wholeheartedly. She knew that it would be difficult for either Grant or Rebekah to get away to attend, so she willingly went in their place and promised to take notes.

In Josie's opinion, the shelter director was the most "together" woman she had ever encountered and she gladly took the woman up on her suggestion.

Still, Josie did have some concerns. "Are you sure no one will mind my attending this gathering?" she asked as Bethany drove them over to the meeting. "I'm not even married anymore."

"No, but you are helping take care of twins," Bethany pointed out. "The sort of knowledge you can pick up at the meeting will definitely come in very handy. Remember, you're not just doing this for yourself, you're doing it for Grant and Rebekah, not to mention Lucas and Lily," the woman added.

Put that way, Josie couldn't very well disagree with the director.

She happily attended the meeting.

Josie found the get-together very informative, but what she really enjoyed was seeing the various "survivors" of what she thought of as "the twin invasion." What she also noticed was that the people at the meeting were not all couples.

"C'mon," Bethany coaxed once the meeting was over, "I want to introduce you to Ian Parson."

Hooking her arm through Josie's, Bethany drew her best shelter volunteer over toward a slightly frazzled and exhausted-looking young father. The brown-haired, brown-eyed man was holding on to twins that looked to be approximately three years of age. Both girls, one who looked withdrawn and one who gave the impression that she was a regular live wire.

"Ian," Bethany greeted the young man, "I'd like you to meet Josie Whitaker."

The athletically built father turned toward the woman he had just been introduced to. Since each of his hands was attached to one of the twins, he could only nod his head by way of a greeting.

"Hello, sorry my hands are a little occupied," he said. There was a note of wistful envy in his voice. He clearly loved his twins, but one way or another, they appeared to definitely be a handful for him.

"It's okay. I'm used to the way twins take up both hands," she explained. "I spend a lot of time looking after my twin niece and nephew."

"Brave lady," Ian commented. "We'll be leaving in a few minutes, Abby," he said to his more rambunctious daughter. "Calm down." He looked back to Josie. "What do your brother and sister-in-law have?" he asked, struggling to keep Abby still.

The other little girl, Josie couldn't help noticing, didn't give the impression that she was listening at all. She stood gazing off at the people leaving their seats.

"Lucas and Lily. A boy and a girl," Josie added after the fact.

"You might think I have a matched set," Ian told her needlessly. "But their personalities are worlds apart," he added, looking at Bethany. "As you can tell, one daughter is very outgoing while the other is almost terminally shy. Right now, I'm hoping that they wind up rubbing off on one another at least a little," Ian confided.

The squirmy one had enough energy for two people, Josie thought. "Does it get any easier with time?" she wanted to know.

"Sure," he answered without any conviction. "People tell me that'll happen in another twenty-five years or so, but then another whole new set of problems will probably settle in. My advice to your brother and sister-in-law is to take it one day at a time," Ian told her. "Getting through a whole day in one piece is an accomplishment in itself. The only thing I managed to learn in all this time," Ian confided to the two women, "is that one and one do not make two. It makes a crowd. Tell them the sooner they get used to that, the better."

"Oh, you know you wouldn't trade places with anyone else for the world," Bethany told him.

"You're right," Ian agreed. "But that's because by the end of the day, between my engineering job and the twins, I'm too worn out to put one foot in front of the other to get away, so trading places is completely out of the question."

The man made it sound as if it was just him tackling the situation, Josie thought. That didn't seem right to her.

"Is your wife able to spend any time with the twins?" she asked.

The moment she began to ask the question, Josie could see Bethany shaking her head at her, mouthing the words *Don't ask him about his wife.* But it was obviously too late.

The look on Ian's face almost ripped her heart out. She had never seen that much sadness in a human being before.

"My wife, Serena, got sick soon after the twins were born," he told her. "She died when they were eighteen months old. My mother-in-law is helping out for the moment while I'm working." Reflecting on what he had just said, he added, "Except that she criticizes everything I do." Ian flushed. "That had to sound ungrateful," he realized. "I guess I shouldn't have said that," the twins' father apologized.

"I'm very sorry—for your loss and for the criticism you've had to put up with," Josie said, remembering what she had had to put up with when her ex-husband decided to take off. There were people she knew who just assumed he had left because of something *she* had done. "Sometimes people who mean well don't know how to express themselves," she told him, hoping that would comfort him a little.

"I suppose you're right," Ian replied.

Maybe it was her imagination, but she didn't think that he sounded all that convinced.

"Well, thanks for talking to me," Josie said, offering Ian a smile as she and Bethany began to leave.

Ian nodded, although his attention was already focused back on his twins. "Don't mention it," he murmured, going in the opposite direction.

"That poor man," Josie sympathized.

Bethany nodded. "I know. I suppose that just goes to show you that there's always someone out there who's even worse off than you think you are," the director said, speaking in general terms.

"I'll say," Josie wholeheartedly agreed. Her sympathy had been aroused. She felt awful for the man. "Do you know what his wife died of?" she asked Bethany.

"Cancer," the woman told her simply. "Serena thought she was just exhausted all the time because having the twins took so much out of her. By the time they felt that she should see a doctor in case it turned out to be something else, it was already too late." Bethany pressed her lips together.

"How awful," Josie cried, meaning the words from the very bottom of her soul. "Maybe I should suggest that Grant and Rebekah get together with Ian and his twins. It might be good for all of them," she speculated, thinking out loud.

"That sounds like a really good idea," Bethany replied. "Ian could certainly use the company. Right now, that poor man is working himself to death—if he doesn't wind up expiring from a broken heart."

It was Rebekah who noticed that despite being busy taking care of the twins and working at the animal shelter with Shannon, as well as doing plenty of baking and keeping up with what was now an occasional riding lesson with Declan, Josie didn't seem quite as happy as usual.

Part of her felt as if she shouldn't be butting in, but then, family was family and Josie hadn't sat on the sidelines when she'd felt that they needed her.

She had volunteered her services before they'd ever asked for her help.

"Is anything wrong, Josie?" Rebekah asked her sister-in-law after putting her twins down for a nap. When Josie looked at her quizzically, Rebekah said, "You look a little down lately."

Josie was about to shrug off the question, but then decided that she had always been honest with her brother and sister-in-law and that now wasn't the time to suddenly shift gears.

"Well, I realized that you and Grant are getting things more under control these days, taking care of the twins and all—which is great, I'm really happy for you," she added quickly. "But Bethany has been officially installed as the permanent shelter director, which means there's no pressure for you to go back, so it doesn't seem as if I'm all that necessary any more. Maybe there's no longer any real urgent need for me to stick around town. I suppose I could always just go back to Florida," Josie said.

The thought left her less than happy. She frowned, looking over at her sister-in-law. "But to be totally honest, the thought of leaving here does make me feel extremely sad," Josie admitted.

Rebekah sat down next to her sister-in-law. "Grant and I were just talking about how great it was to have you so close by. You're like our own personal guardian angel," she told her. She leaned in closer to Josie as if the closeness emphasized her point. "You know you are more than welcome to stay in that apartment over the garage for as long as you want.

"Longer," she emphasized the next moment. "I can't think of anything better than to have the twins grow up having their aunt Josie around, looking after them, teaching them things, playing with them. If you *want* to go," Rebekah told her, "we won't stand in your way. But if you don't have your heart set on leaving, we would *love* to have you stay here with us."

Josie offered her sister-in-law a wide smile. "I guess I'll stay then."

The latter all but squealed as she hugged Josie. "Wonderful!" she exclaimed happily, honestly relieved to have her sister-in-law agreeing to remain— for so many reasons.

Josie was definitely happy to have her life fall into place this way. For the time being, she stopped worrying if she should stay or leave.

In this frame of mind, she swung by Declan's ranch the following afternoon to pick Shannon up before going to the animal shelter.

Shannon couldn't wait to go.

As was her habit, Josie had prepared a late lunch to take with her for some of the volunteers working at the shelter.

Dropping Shannon off so the girl could work with some of the shyer dogs, Josie brought in the lunches and distributed them. Once that was done, she went to see Bethany in her office. She was looking forward to spending a little time just talking to the woman before she went back to help Shannon with the dogs.

But things didn't quite work out the way she had hoped.

Josie found the director in her office looking very upset. Her usually smooth brow was furrowed as she sat at her desk looking over a spreadsheet that was laid out in front of her.

Considering how upbeat the woman normally was, seeing her looking this way was something quite unusual and unsettling in Josie's opinion.

Even though the door was open, Josie didn't venture in. Instead she knocked lightly on the door jamb. When Bethany didn't look up, Josie knocked again, a little louder this time.

Blinking, Bethany seemed to snap out of her mental reverie. Looking up, she seemed to see Josie for the first time.

"I'm sorry," the woman apologized. "Were you standing there long?"

"Not long," Josie brushed off. "But I did knock," she pointed out. "You didn't seem to hear me." She entered, drawing closer to the director. The woman did look upset. "Is there something wrong?"

"Nothing a wheelbarrow full of money couldn't fix," the director quipped sadly.

"I think we're all in that boat," Josie said, placing the lunch she had prepared for the shelter director in front of her. "Could you be a little more specific?" she requested.

Josie really wanted to help, but to do that, she needed to understand what the actual problem was.

"Well, to start with, there are the four German shepherds from that backyard breeding operation—they were really sick," Bethany said, sifting through a pile of papers that consisted of various medical bills that the four dogs had incurred.

Josie nodded. "I remember. I was here when they were brought in," she reminded the woman.

"Three of those dogs are now recovering," Bethany told her. "We'll be able to move them into the Pets for Vets program." She sighed, looking at another bill. "All of them except for Jedidiah," she said.

"He's not doing well?" Josie asked sympathetically.

Bethany shook her head. "No. He's still recovering from pneumonia and the poor thing is still pretty weak," the director said. "But Jedidiah isn't the only problem."

Josie studied the director's face. She didn't look happy. "I take it there's more?" Josie asked. Bethany nodded her head but didn't share any more details. "What is it?" Josie pressed the director.

Maybe if she talked about it, some new possibility would occur to her, Bethany thought.

"Well, we also took in a lot of puppies, all of who need to be fed and taken care of. Money is flowing out like water, but there isn't much flowing back in. Donations are down," she said, sighing. "And, frankly, I'm not sure what to do."

"I'm guessing that bank robbery is out," Josie wisecracked.

Bethany's eyes met hers. Her smile was incredibly sad. "I'm afraid so."

"Well, there's got to be something we can do," Josie told the director with determination. "Let me think about it for a little while. I'll let you know if I come up with something," she said.

Bethany laughed sadly under her breath. "I'd appreciate it," she said, getting back to the budget she had drawn up. It didn't look any better now than when she had initially filled in the figures.

"In the meantime, you need to keep your strength up," Josie told her, pushing the lunch closer to the woman. "Eat!" she ordered just before she walked out.

Chapter Thirteen

"I was beginning to think that maybe you'd lost interest in horseback riding lessons," Declan said when Josie showed up at his stable for another lesson.

Several days had gone by at this point and he was fairly certain he had scared her off after he had given in to the extremely strong urge that had come over him that morning by the lake.

Though he hadn't regretted kissing her, he had felt bad about scaring her off. Although apologies had always been next to impossible for him, he was relieved that he didn't need to try to find the words.

"Oh no, I didn't lose interest," Josie told him as she began to saddle Marigold. "Unfortunately, a lot of things came up in the last few days and I've just been too busy to take the time to indulge myself."

"Indulge yourself?" Declan questioned. "How's that again?"

Moving quickly, he saddled his stallion in half the time that it took Josie to saddle her mare.

"Well, these riding lessons are just for me," she explained, tightening the mare's cinch. "Everything else that takes up my time is either for my brother and his wife, or the twins, or your niece, or someone else. Even working at the animal rescue shelter actually focuses on the animals.

"Don't get me wrong," she told him quickly. "I love doing all of those things, but none of them are strictly for myself. There are always other people involved. But when I go for a riding lesson," she concluded with a smile, "that's strictly just for me. I see it as an indulgence, which makes it hard for me to justify if there's something else for me to do."

Declan led his horse out of the stable as he absorbed this information. Could this woman actually be that selfless? "Oh."

Josie couldn't tell by his tone of voice if he had his doubts about what she had just said, or if he was thinking about what had happened between them during her last lesson and felt she was just being coy. There were a lot of ways to interpret the single word he had uttered.

Just when had things gotten to be so complicated? she couldn't help wondering.

Declan swung into his saddle. "You ready?" he asked, looking down from on top of his stallion.

Gripping the saddle horn, Josie swung up into the

saddle. Not as smoothly as Declan had, but she was getting better, she thought happily.

"Ready," she declared.

"Then let's go," he told her just before he applied his heels to the stallion's flanks.

Less than a second later, he was off.

The last time Declan had taken off like that, he had caught her off guard and she'd wound up trailing behind him.

But not this time, she promised herself. Josie was totally determined to keep pace with the rugged cowboy.

They ended up riding neck and neck like that until they had gone several miles. At that point, Declan raised his hand, signaling that they needed to stop and rest for a few minutes.

"You're wearing out the horses, not to mention me," her instructor told her with a hint of a smile.

Bringing his horse to a stop, Declan dismounted, then started to reach for Marigold's reins. But it was at exactly that moment that a snake slithered in front of Marigold, instantly spooking the mare. Rather than coming to a halt, the mare took off at full gallop.

At first, Declan thought that Josie was just trying to show off. But he quickly realized that the mare had taken off at breakneck speed on her own. If the horse stopped suddenly, Josie was in imminent danger of being thrown and landing on the ground on her back—or worse.

Declan's instincts took over. Kicking Midnight's flanks, he urged his stallion to a full gallop. He knew that Midnight was faster than Marigold. Even though the latter had a head start, he knew he could catch the mare.

"Looks like we've got a rescue on our hands," he said to his stallion. Raising his voice, he called out to Josie. "Hang on!"

"I'm trying to," Josie shouted back over her shoulder, doing her best not to lean one way or the other. She was well aware that the slightest miscalculation on her part could cause her to take a damaging fall.

Her heart was in her throat as Marigold continued to bolt down the trail. Josie had no idea that Declan's stallion was capable of running as fast as he was.

Midnight was flying, cutting the distance between them. Within moments, horse and rider managed to catch up to Marigold.

Once Midnight was side by side with Josie's very spooked mare, Declan leaned forward, waiting for his chance. Spurring his stallion on, the breeder was finally able to reach out and catch hold of Josie's waist.

In what seemed like a very fluid movement, Declan pulled her off her horse and onto his.

Holding on to her tightly, Declan had seated Josie precariously in front of him. That was when he brought Midnight to an eventual halt.

His own heart was pounding. So many things could have gone wrong. "Are you all right?" he asked the woman he was holding against him.

"I'm winded, but yes, I'm fine," she answered in a short, breathless gasp.

That was all he wanted to hear. "I'm going to set you down and go after Marigold. Don't go anywhere," he warned.

Like she could walk, Josie thought as her feet touched the ground.

"I won't," she promised, still trying to catch her breath. "Don't forget to come back."

Declan just laughed as he took off after the runaway mare.

Her legs were feeling weak after her ordeal. Josie sank down on the ground and looked around.

She had no idea where she was. If for some reason, she needed to walk home from here, she had no doubt that it would be an almost impossible undertaking.

Looking around again, Josie searched for some sort of point of orientation, something that would tell her where she was. But she couldn't find anything familiar.

How did natives of the area have any sense of where they were? It seemed like an impossible ordeal to her.

Still feeling somewhat shaky, Josie rose to her feet. *I can do this*, she told herself. *I can do this*. Besides, she thought, Declan would be back any minute now.

Trying not to worry or dwell on any stories about the sort of misadventures that could easily befall Declan or herself, Josie continued looking around. She was hoping to catch a glimpse of either of the horses.

It felt as if an eternity had gone by, even though she knew that it hadn't.

Finally, just as she was beginning to think that something had happened and Declan wasn't coming back, Josie heard the sound of hoofbeats.

She offered up a prayer of thanksgiving even before she could make out either one of the horses—or even if it actually was Declan that she saw riding toward her.

The rider and the horse he was on, not to mention the one he was leading behind him, were approaching her at what seemed like a pretty leisurely pace.

Why? Josie couldn't help wondering.

The next moment, she was able to make out both horses as well as the rider.

Declan! she thought in relief.

That was when she let out the breath she wasn't even aware of holding. It sounded incredibly shaky to her ear, as if she couldn't get enough oxygen in.

"You came back," she cried happily as she ran up to horse and rider.

"Didn't you think I would?" Declan asked her in disbelief. "I said I'd be back," he reminded her.

She didn't appear to be disoriented, but maybe that overly fast ride had gotten to her more than he had realized, Declan thought.

"I was worried," she confessed then gestured around the area. "Everything looks the same. How did you know where I was?"

Declan thought she was kidding as he looked at her. "You're serious," he realized, dismounting. He looked at her. "That's like asking me how I breathe. I just do," he told her. "No thought is really required."

Josie shrugged. "I'm a city girl," she reminded her instructor. "Finding my way around in the wilderness doesn't come naturally to me."

"Orienting yourself to your surroundings is part of the riding lessons," he told her, then assured her, "Don't worry, it'll all come to you eventually."

Declan made it sound as if he believed that she was going to live here in Spring Forest permanently. That was when she realized that, despite her talk with Rebekah earlier, she was still vacillating as to whether or not she would remain.

Not wanting to get into that, she just said, "If you say so." Then, changing the subject, she asked Declan, "Do you know what spooked Marigold like that? She's usually so calm."

At the moment, Marigold was standing beside Midnight. The mare looked completely relaxed. It was as if she had imagined the whole wild ride across the meadow.

Except that she knew she hadn't.

"It could have been any one of a number of things," he told her. "A rabbit, a gopher, maybe even a snake. I didn't see what it was myself, but any one of those suddenly popping up in front of her could send Marigold on her way. Midnight doesn't spook," Declan said, "but Midnight's the exception, not the rule." He looked closely at Josie, concerned. "You didn't get hurt, did you?" he wanted to know.

"Now that I think about it, I did pull you off Marigold pretty roughly."

"I'm not complaining. I would have been hurt a lot more if you hadn't pulled me off when you did," Josie told him.

He liked the fact Josie realized that, and that she wasn't complaining that he had pulled her off as roughly as he now realized he had. If that had happened to any of the handful of other students he had instructed over the last year, he had no doubt they would have carried on and on about how much it had hurt them.

"You're a good sport, Josie," Declan told her, surprising her with the compliment. His next words surprised her even more. "And you're really learning how to handle yourself on a horse. A lot of other students I've worked with would have wound up hitting the ground when Marigold got spooked and took off. You could have even gotten trampled."

"Guess I was just lucky," she responded.

"Luck had very little to do with it," Declan said with conviction. "You're getting to be a very good rider," he told her. "And I don't say that to just anyone," the man added. "When you get home," he continued, "I'd suggest that you soak in a hot tub because you're going to ache like hell tomorrow," he predicted.

That didn't make any sense to her. "But I didn't fall off," she reminded him. Although, now that she thought about it, her ribs did ache a little because of the way he had grabbed her.

"No, but you bounced around on Marigold like a regular rag doll as she galloped through the field," Declan pointed out. "That has consequences."

She nodded. "Hot tub. Soaking. Got it," Josie recited.

"Do you feel up to riding back?" he asked her, debating telling her that they could wait a while. He didn't like the idea of causing her more pain.

Josie smiled. "It certainly beats walking," she answered.

He couldn't argue with that. "Okay, then let's go," he told her.

She went to mount her horse and found that her legs just couldn't make it up and over. Embarrassed, Josie tried again. And wound up failing again.

At a loss, Josie wasn't sure what to do when she suddenly felt very strong hands against her posterior, giving her that extra boost, just like the first time she had mounted Marigold.

"Sorry," Declan apologized, circling around to mount his own horse. He was referring to the fact that he'd had to give her that extra push to get her up on Marigold. He had tried his best to keep the contact from being intimate. "That seemed to be the fastest way to get you up on your horse."

"I understand and I'm not complaining," she told him. There was no point to doing that. For one thing, it was after the fact. For another, she had momentarily been willing to go a lot further than that at the lake that time.

"No," he agreed, nodding his head. "You're not. That's why you make such a good student."

Picking up his reins, Declan looked at her. His voice was almost gentle as he asked her, "Are you ready, or would you feel better if I held on to Marigold's reins as we go back?"

The question caught her completely off guard. "Isn't there a saying about getting back on the horse that threw you?" she asked.

Declan's mouth curved, deeply this time. "There is," he answered.

"Then I'm back on the horse and I'm ready," she told him.

Josie threaded Marigold's reins through her fingers, making sure that the mare didn't have enough slack to encourage her to take off again. Although, she reasoned, the chances of that happening twice in one day went from incredibly slim to nonexistent.

"Don't be in a hurry to get back to the stable," Declan counseled. "Marigold was spooked. If she senses that you're tense as well, that could make her twice as skittish. Just act as if nothing's happened. She needs to be calmed, and horses are pretty intuitive. They can easily pick up on whatever you're going through and act on it."

Her head hurt and it had nothing to do with the jolt she had received while bouncing around on Marigold's back. Right now it felt as if all her thoughts were being shuffled.

"That's an awful lot to remember," she told Declan. "I'm not sure I can keep it all straight," Josie confessed.

It amazed him that he had faith in her, but he did. "You'd be surprised," he promised her. "All this will become second nature to you before you know it."

"I certainly would be surprised," she told him.

Declan nodded at the way she was holding the reins. "Don't hold on to Marigold's reins so tightly," he advised. "Loosen your grip."

"Won't she take off if I *don't* hold on to her reins?" she asked.

"She's more likely to take off if she feels that there's too much tension in the reins," he told her.

"I held on tightly to the reins before," Josie pointed out.

He knew she was referring to that first day. "Yes, but that was just a regular day and you were both getting used to each other. Don't make her feel that you're afraid she might repeat her flight. Relax," he urged. "It's going to be all right."

Josie released the breath she was holding. "If you say so," she said.

Declan smiled ever so slightly and nodded his head. "I do," he answered.

They returned to the stable without any further incident.

Dismounting, they led their respective horses back into their stalls.

"I can take care of your horse if you just want to get home," Declan offered.

"Stop being so nice," she told her instructor. "You're going to throw me off."

He laughed under his breath. "Can't have that." He waited until he removed the stallion's saddle then asked Josie, "So, when do you want to come back for the next lesson?"

"The day after tomorrow?" she asked, prepared to be turned down. Declan had always waited at least four days between sessions, if not longer.

"Sounds good to me," he told her.

Josie didn't realize that she was smiling so widely until she caught her reflection in the water that was standing in the bucket in Marigold's stall. Raising her eyes, she saw that Declan was looking at her. Apparently, they had gotten to another, more comfortable plateau.

She made no effort to stop smiling. If anything, her smile just widened.

Chapter Fourteen

The last thing Josie suggested to him at the end of her lesson was that he might pick up a few books for Shannon. Josie had thought the girl might welcome some reading about shelter animals to help her properly work with the dogs at the shelter. The more he thought about it, the more Declan warmed to the idea.

That was why he decided to go into town and stop by the local bookstore, Chapter One, the following day. Although he didn't go into town all that often, Declan was aware that the bookstore had changed hands less than a year ago. Word had it that Chapter One been purchased by Lucy Tucker who was herself a recent transplant from the neighboring North Carolina city of Charlotte.

As Declan approached the store, he couldn't help overhearing the sound of raised voices. Apparently, Lucy was in the middle of a rather serious conversation with someone. Even though he tried not to listen, Declan thought he recognized the other voice as belonging to Calum Ramsey. Calum was the owner of Pins and Pints, the local bowling alley located one door down from the bookstore.

Declan neither liked nor believed in eavesdropping, but it was rather difficult for him to tune out the raised voices since he had literally walked in on the duo.

Lucy and Calum seemed to be involved in some sort of loud disagreement.

As the door abruptly closed behind him, Lucy and Calum turned almost in unison to look at the man who had just walked in.

Caught, Declan cleared his throat. "Um, sorry. I didn't mean to interrupt you. I'll just go and come back later," he offered.

Lucy, a very pretty young woman with light brown skin, recognized the man who had come in. She was quick to absolve the customer of any sort of wrongdoing.

"That's all right. There's nothing to apologize for," she told Declan, saying, "We were just talking." She glanced back at Calum. "Maybe a little more passionately than either one of us realized," the bookstore owner allowed.

"Right. What she said," Calum told Declan, embarrassed to be caught like this. He began edging toward the front door. "Well, I'd better be going any-way," he said, avoiding Lucy's expressive dark brown eyes. "Stop by for a beer sometime. Or maybe a game," he told Declan just as he left the shop.

Declan nodded, echoing, "Sometime," although it was already too late for Calum to have heard him. The man was gone.

Even though Calum had absolved him of any blame, Declan couldn't help feeling that he had walked in on something he shouldn't have. The prob-lem was, he wasn't sure exactly what that was, or how to actually word his apology.

To his way of thinking, the best way to proceed was just to fall back on the reason he had come here in the first place. Turning toward Lucy, he was just about to ask the bookstore owner if she had any ap-propriate nonfiction books on caring for animals that he could buy and give to his fourteen-year-old niece.

However, it seemed that Lucy had other ideas at the moment. She immediately latched onto Declan's arm and began to draw him over toward her office, which was located at the back of the store.

"Have you met my foster dog, Buttercup?" she asked, smiling brightly at Declan.

Since he felt that his presence had managed to chase Calum away for some reason, Declan didn't feel right about turning the woman down outright, at least not immediately.

"No, I haven't," he told her, sensing that it wouldn't end with that.

"She's wonderful—although, of course, she's needed some special care," she told Declan.

He wasn't really sure what she was talking about. But the fastest way to find out was to ask, so he did. "What do you mean?"

The words were no sooner out of Declan's mouth than he saw *exactly* what she was referring to. Buttercup, a golden retriever, was lying on a soft blue blanket. She was also very visibly pregnant.

"I'm so excited for the puppies to come," Lucy said. "But I've already started the process of trying to find good homes for them once they arrive." She raised her eyes hopefully and asked, "Would you be interested?"

Declan in turn looked at the placid, fluffy mama. "She's very cute," he told Lucy. "And I'm sure her puppies will be, too."

She could detect hesitation in his voice. She was very familiar with that by now. "I hear a 'but' in your voice, Declan."

He saw no reason to lie. "Very astute," the breeder remarked. "I already have a dog. His name is Champ," he told her. "He's a one-man dog and I get the feeling that if I take in a puppy, that puppy will have to watch his or her back *all* the time. Champ doesn't care for competition and he's pretty jealous, not to mention protective when it comes to me."

Lucy nodded. She had already begun to suspect something like that.

"Well, I had to ask," she told him.

"I understand," Declan answered. "Now, about

the books I'm looking for..." he said, getting back to the reason he had stopped by the bookstore to begin with.

"Of course," Lucy said. "Let's get out of my office and back to the bookstore proper." As she closed her office door behind her, she looked up at her customer. "It goes without saying that if you happen to run into anyone looking to acquire an adorable puppy, you will steer them in my direction," she told him.

Declan decided not to mention the fact that his niece as well as his riding student were both putting in time at the animal shelter. Saying that seemed too much like willfully dashing the poor woman's hopes.

So instead, Declan just nodded his head. "If I happen to run into anyone," he promised, "I'll definitely send them your way."

"Thank you," Lucy responded with a smile. "Now, about those books you were looking to buy."

"Josie," Ruth said, looking up from the tea she was brewing. She had just heard Josie's voice as the latter called out to her granddaughter. "Didn't I hear you tell Shannon that you used to own a catering company when you lived back in Florida?"

As had become her habit, Josie had stopped at the Hoyt house to pick up Shannon before going to the animal shelter.

Hearing the young woman greet Shannon, Ruth came out to talk to her before Josie could leave with her granddaughter.

Used to own.

Even though she was still thinking about relocating permanently, it was difficult for Josie to think of her catering business in the past tense. To her it was a very viable part of her life.

"Yes, I did," she deliberately added.

Ruth didn't seem to hear the qualifying statement. Instead, she just pushed on, focusing on the fact that Josie had run a catering company.

"Well, I have a proposition for you," Declan's mother told his student.

"And that would be?" Josie politely asked. She, as well as Shannon, were due at the shelter, but she was not about to cut Ruth off. So, she politely waited to hear what this "proposition" was all about.

"Well, I have a friend of a friend," Ruth began, unraveling her story slowly. "Her name is Regina Mackenzie. Regina periodically throws charitable events for local organizations," Declan's mother added, looking at Josie to see if her words were making an impression.

Josie nodded politely. She had heard the woman's name mentioned before though their paths had never crossed. "Yes, I know."

Ruth began to get warmed up. "Well, I told her all about you."

Josie didn't really understand why Ruth would mention her to the other woman at all. "Why would you do that?" she asked.

Ruth began getting excited. "Her caterer got sick and the woman is not going to be able to cater this latest soiree that Regina is throwing this Saturday and it's too late to call it off. All the invitations have already gone out." Ruth drew closer. "I was wondering if you would be able to step in and, you know, save the day by handling the catering for her," Ruth suggested hopefully. "You'd be a real lifesaver," she told Josie with feeling. "And it would mean the world to Regina. Regina is a very good friend to have," Declan's mother added. "She has a lot of influence in this town. Do you think you can do it on such short notice?"

Josie bit her lower lip. Her life was already extremely busy. Quite honestly, she felt that she really didn't have any free time to spare.

But the truth of it was, if she *was* looking to start a new catering business here in Spring Forest, this sort of thing would be the perfect opportunity to begin building her reputation.

She already had a small head start because of the biscotti she was selling at the coffee shop in response to the owner's request.

"Yes," Josie finally answered, nodding her head. "I can do it."

"Wonderful!" Ruth declared happily. If her hands hadn't hurt as much as they had, she would have clapped them together in celebration. As far as the woman was concerned, it was a done deal. She was glad to be able to facilitate things for the younger woman who had made such a difference in her son's and granddaughter's life.

Josie's mind was already racing, thinking about all the preparations she needed to make by this coming Saturday. But she had promised Shannon that they were going to go to the rescue shelter today and she wasn't the type to just go back on her word.

Not to mention the fact that Bethany was expecting her there as well.

"Okay, Shannon, we've got to get going," Josie told the teenager, beginning to usher her toward the front door.

"We're still going?" Shannon asked in surprise. She had thought that because of what her grandmother had just said, their outing would be called off.

"You bet we are," Josie told the girl with feeling. "It might be our last time for a few days, but we definitely are going today."

Even as she said that to Shannon, an idea suddenly occurred to Josie. This unexpected catering gig might lead to something else as well.

"Thank you for the recommendation," she told Ruth just before she and Shannon left.

"My pleasure entirely," Ruth called after her, happily beaming over the way that everything was turning out.

By the time she and Shannon had arrived at the animal shelter, Josie had worked out most of the details in her mind. Not about the catering gig itself, since she'd need to talk to Regina about what she wanted, but about what it could yield if she went about this in the right way.

But first, she knew she needed to run this all by Bethany.

After dropping off Shannon where the puppies were being kept so the teenager could continue working with them, especially with Harlow who the teen couldn't stop talking about, Josie made a point of stopping by Bethany's office. The director looked just as crestfallen as she had the other day.

"Things no better than they were the other day?" she asked the other woman.

Bethany raised her eyes from the spreadsheet that had been giving her such headaches. Try as she might, she couldn't find any extra money, or any solutions to her dilemma.

"If anything, the situation is even worse than before. Two more strays have been dropped off at the shelter since I talked to you the last time." She sighed, rubbing the area just above her eyes. There was a very intense headache building up.

"Luckily, they don't need any extra medical care beyond the usual checkup, shots and neutering," Bethany said. "But I don't even have enough money for that, much less the money for the outstanding medical bills we already have." She raised her head to look at Josie. "I really don't know what I'm going to do," she confessed helplessly.

"How about having a fundraiser?" Josie suggested eagerly.

"That would be great, but that kind of thing takes a bit of doing," Bethany told her. "I don't have the time. That's not just something that you can pull out of a hat at will."

According to what Ruth had already told her and

what she'd heard around town, Regina Mackenzie had a wonderful reputation for throwing very successful fundraisers. The woman enjoyed putting her name behind good causes—and this could definitely be classified as a good cause.

"Leave it to me," Josie happily told the director. "I've got an idea how we can find that money you need for the animals."

For the first time since she had walked in on the woman several days ago, Josie saw Bethany looking really hopeful.

"What sort of an idea?" Bethany wanted to know.

"One that can help provide the funds for those mounting bills you were attempting to juggle." Josie patted the woman's shoulder. "Let me see what I can do," she told the director.

"You're not going to tell me, are you?" Bethany guessed.

"Not until I can see if I can get this fundraiser off the ground," Josie told the woman. She didn't want to raise Bethany's hopes until she was certain she could get Regina interested in this proposition.

"You're being extremely mysterious," Bethany told Josie.

"I prefer to think of it as being overly cautious," Josie replied. "Don't worry, I'll let you know the moment I make any progress with this," she promised.

To her surprise, the director rose from her chair. Rounding her desk, Bethany actually hugged her.

"I haven't done anything yet, Bethany," Josie pointed out.

"I know." Bethany dropped her hands, but she remained standing beside Josie. "That was just to thank you for trying."

Later that day, as Josie drove back to Declan's house to drop Shannon off, she thought about what she was going to say to Regina once they'd connected. She just assumed, since this had been Ruth's suggestion, that Declan's mother had paved the way for her and had touched base with the woman, but she wasn't entirely sure that she wasn't just taking things for granted.

The moment she climbed up the stairs to her small upstairs apartment, Josie placed a call to Regina.

The phone rang a number of times before it was picked up. Josie half expected to find herself talking to either an answering machine or possibly a secretary, since Ruth had told her how very busy the woman usually was.

Instead, Josie heard a clipped voice on the other end say, "Yes?"

She had no idea what the woman sounded like so, nervously, she asked, "Is this Ms. Regina Mackenzie?"

Rather than confirm her identity, Regina ordered, "Talk quickly, I'm in the middle of searching for a caterer," the woman on the other end told her.

So, the woman hadn't found another one yet. *Score one for me*, Josie thought.

"Ruth Hoyt gave me your number. I'm an established caterer from Florida and she just told me that your caterer got sick. If you'd let me, I'd like to offer my services," Josie told the woman.

There was no hesitation, no long litany of questions. Instead, Regina simply asked her, "How soon before you can get here?"

"Would tomorrow morning be all right?" Josie asked the woman.

"Today would be better," the woman replied authoritatively.

Not waiting for her caller to answer, Regina rattled off her address, then informed Josie, "I'll be waiting," before the connection terminated.

Stunned, Josie stared at the phone before she put the receiver away.

Chapter Fifteen

Josie would have really preferred to meet with Regina in the morning. A night's rest would have gone a long way toward getting her some clarity. As it was, when she arrived at Regina's house, she had to admit that she was somewhat unsettled and nervous.

How bad could it be? she asked herself. If this interview—she couldn't think of it as anything else—actually went badly, she'd be no worse off than she was now, right? And if she managed to impress the woman, she would at least wind up landing the gig. And who knew? If that happened, she knew that she could very well go on to become Regina's backup caterer if not her actual go-to caterer. From the little bit she had picked up from Ruth, Regina Mackenzie threw these fundraising parties all the time.

Regina's house was breathtaking, Josie thought as she approached the large colonial building's front door. Throwing her shoulders back, she rang the doorbell.

The sound of chimes echoed back to her, but the door remained closed. It took a second attempt on her part before the door finally opened. When it did, Josie found herself looking at a thin, young woman who looked to be about five foot five and around twenty-five years of age. The young woman looked at her quizzically.

Josie cleared her throat. "I'm not sure if I'm at the right address," she said, trying to explain her presence. "I'm looking for Regina Mackenzie."

"You're at the right address," the stranger confirmed, opening the front door further to admit Josie. "Regina Mackenzie is my aunt," she said. "I'm Elise Mackenzie. You're the caterer, right? We'll probably be working together. My aunt likes me to keep track of things when she's throwing one of her fundraisers. She throws a lot of fundraisers," Elise added as she ushered Josie inside, "so it's easy for her to get all those details confused.

"She's waiting for you. Come with me," Elise urged. Turning, she led the way back to her aunt's office.

Stopping before a closed ornate mahogany door, Elise knocked lightly then walked in. She glanced over her shoulder, beckoning for Josie to follow.

"Aunt Regina, this is the caterer you've been waiting to meet," Elise said. The next moment, the young woman promptly melted into the background.

Josie took that as her cue. Extending her hand toward the stately, well-dressed woman, she began to introduce herself. "Hello, I'm—"

"Josie Whitaker, yes, I know," Regina said, nodding in acknowledgment. Gesturing to the chair in front of her desk, Regina instructed, "Take a seat."

Josie did as she was told, as did, she noticed, Regina's niece. The latter sat on the edge of her seat, looking for all the world as if she couldn't get comfortable anywhere.

As for Regina, the woman appeared to look exactly as she had envisioned her, Josie thought. She was stylishly dressed, looking very regal. Regina had a take-charge manner about her that seemed to fill the room she was in. Josie had a feeling it was like that in every room the woman walked into.

Not knowing what to expect, Josie waited for the woman to speak first and take charge of their meeting. She didn't have long to wait.

"You have a very good record," Regina said as she leaned forward.

Josie looked slightly taken aback. "How would you know that?" She hadn't given the woman a résumé or anything.

"I have my connections," Regina told her loftily. "But I noticed that you have only catered small parties. My one question to you is can you handle a soiree for over a hundred people?"

The thought did create butterflies in Josie's stomach, but she managed to confidently answer, "No problem."

Regina nodded her approval. "Confidence, I like that. Elise can connect you with all the suppliers you're going to need for this. Just give her a list."

Turning, the woman looked at her niece. "Elise, give Ms. Whitaker the guest list and fill her in on my guests' preferences." Regina leaned back in her chair, her piercing gaze fixed on Josie's face. "I pride myself on how well these things go and especially on how much money I am always able to raise. I'm assuming this will be no different," the woman said with confidence. "Anything you need," she told Josie, waving a hand toward her niece, "just let Elise know."

Josie nodded. "I appreciate that."

"This has to go off like clockwork," Regina informed her new caterer. "The soiree is set for Saturday at three o'clock. Anything else?" the woman asked as she rose to her feet.

It was now or never, Josie thought. Taking a breath, she pressed her lips together then started talking. "You have a wonderful reputation as a fundraiser, Ms. Mackenzie…" Josie began.

Regina arched a quizzical eyebrow. "Yes?" she asked expectantly.

Josie jumped in with both feet. "I also put time in at the Furever Paws Animal Rescue."

Regina nodded regally. "I am aware of that. I like to know exactly who I am hiring," she told the younger woman. She wasn't bragging, she was stating a simple fact.

It was the lead in that Josie was looking for. "Then you're probably aware of the fact that the shelter has been taking in more than its share of strays lately. Funds are being stretched to the limit," Josie told the woman. "Beyond the limit, actually."

Regina nodded, knowing where this was leading. "And you find yourself in need of a fundraiser," the woman concluded.

"Yes, I—" Again, Josie wasn't able to get any further.

"Say no more," Regina instructed. "I'll see what I can do," the woman promised. "In the meantime," she went on, "I expect you to take care of this catering assignment for me. No mishaps," she warned.

She was being given notice that if anything did go wrong, that would be her signal to leave town. And it would certainly be the end of any fundraising hopes for the shelter. "Consider it done," Josie promised.

Regina nodded. "I do."

Whether the woman was paying her a compliment or putting her on notice, Josie had no idea. Maybe this was just a simple proposition of one hand washing the other, she thought.

Mentally, she reached for the soap.

For the next three days, Josie focused her attention almost exclusively on making the preparations for the soiree. Even though Regina Mackenzie had volunteered her niece to take care of all the shopping, Josie preferred to take care of all of that herself. It wasn't a matter of pride, it was a matter of being able to keep track of everything that was going on, as well as stay within the budget Regina had given her for the event.

This way, if she found that she didn't like the products she was looking for in the stores, she could instantly get substitutes or even change the menu.

"But my aunt Regina told me you needed help," Elise protested when she checked in with Josie and the latter had gently turned her away, telling the young woman that she was taking care of getting everything that was needed.

Josie took a closer look at Elise. The brunette seemed incredibly efficient to her, but she also thought that Elise looked extremely exhausted. More so than someone her age should look, she decided.

It was obvious that Elise's aunt was very demanding of the girl's time as well as her energy. Josie could see that all of this was getting to the young woman.

"What I need, Elise," Josie told her gently, "is for you to take a few deep breaths and not have a nervous breakdown." While they didn't look particularly similar, Josie was reminded of her daughter, pushing herself to the limit in college. She made a mental note to call Hannah and check in, maybe convince her to take breaks and get some sleep every now and then.

Did Elise not have anyone in her life to remind her of those things? She was not about to hint that the young woman's aunt was driving her toward this breakdown. If nothing else, that was *not* the right way to solicit Regina's help for the shelter. But she didn't want Elise to drop from exhaustion either.

Without another word, Josie decided to make sure that she was the one who picked up the slack.

Working hard to please this new client, Josie confidently felt that she had everything under control as far as the food went. What she was lacking, however, was the proper space to prepare it all.

Worried, she kept the matter to herself.

However, Declan, of all people, picked up on the fact that Josie was obviously worried about something.

Not someone who danced around issues, he came right out and asked her. "Something wrong?"

Josie didn't want the man thinking of her as a complainer. She was grateful to his mother for helping her get the work. But it all depended on her being able to prepare everything on time, and that looked as if it might not be happening.

Quite frankly, she had no experience with anything of this scale. The smaller events she'd handled up to now had meant that she could manage the cooking in her own kitchen and transport the food in her own car. But that wouldn't make sense here. Her brother's kitchen wasn't big enough to cook for over a hundred people. For the first time since she had gotten into the catering business, Josie actually felt overwhelmed.

"You're not talking," Declan observed when she

didn't answer him. On his way out, he had stopped dead now and was staring at her.

Josie looked up at him blankly.

Declan pressed on. "I asked you if there was something wrong. Your face definitely says yes, so are you going to tell me what it is or are you going to make me have to guess?" he asked. The next moment, he came up with his own answer. "Is this about your catering job? Is it too much for you?" he wanted to know.

"No," Josie denied then amended, "Well, not exactly."

It seemed that he was on the right track, Declan thought. "Then what, exactly?" he persisted.

She might as well tell him. Most likely, he was going to think that she was just complaining, Josie thought. But she couldn't very well avoid answering his question.

"My brother's kitchen isn't big enough for me to do this properly," she told him. "I'd have to cook the food in shifts, which means that it's not all going to be ready—or warm—at the same time."

Declan nodded. He could see how that might be a problem. He came up with a solution. "How do you feel about using my kitchen?"

"Your kitchen?" she echoed, turning the thought over in her head. The size was right, but she would have never been bold enough to ask him to use his kitchen.

"Sure," he answered. "You must have noticed how big it is. I like elbow room when I'm cooking," Declan told her. "That way, I can spread out if I want to. My mom cooks these days," he went on to tell her, "but when her arthritis starts to act up, I'm the one who handles the meals.

"So," he said, coming back to his question since Josie still hadn't given him an answer, "Do you want to use my kitchen or not?"

She was not about to continue second-guessing him. She was just going to assume that he actually meant what he was saying.

"I would love to take you up on your generous offer," Josie told Declan.

"Good," he pronounced, nodding his head. "And, along with the kitchen, I'm throwing in not just one extra set of hands, but two."

"Two?" Josie questioned uncertainly.

"Two," he repeated. "Shannon might not be able to cook like a pro—although she can manage a few things, and you know from the bake sale adventure that she can follow your directions—but she's very good when it comes to carrying trays and serving what's on those trays as well," Declan told her.

"Serving?" she repeated, not sure he meant what she thought he did.

"Sure. The way I see it," Declan explained, "you're going to need help in carting all this food over to where this party is being held, not to mention that you're going to need to have all this food properly laid out and served once you get there with it."

"And you're willing to help with all this?" she couldn't help asking. This was a side of him she'd only caught glimpses of before. Underneath all that brusque exterior, there was definitely a softer, kinder man. Just as she'd always thought.

"Well, you managed to get my niece to act like a human being, which in turn made my mother very happy. So, the way I see it, I owe you for that. Offering you my kitchen, as well as my able body, is the best way I know how to pay you back, since you're too busy these days for riding lessons," Declan told her.

The smile on her face, Declan noted, seemed to light up the whole area.

"I'll take it," Josie happily told him.

"Good," he replied. "Because that's about all I've got to offer. Right now, being in between breeding season, I'm pretty much tapped out monetarily," he told her drolly.

Josie looked at him for a long moment, recalling the kiss they had shared at the lake. That definitely was *not* all he had to offer, she thought. Not with those lips.

Josie abruptly stopped herself before her thoughts took off even more than they already had. She knew thinking like that was only going to lead to complications.

Things hadn't changed, she reminded herself. She was still six years older than Declan, which meant that she was still too old for him, couldn't give him the future he deserved.

But knowing that didn't change the way he could

heat her blood practically to the boiling point just by putting his lips on hers.

"So," he was saying, "you just need to tell me when you're going to need my kitchen and when you want Shannon and me to help bring the cooked food to its destination."

Coming out of her trance, Josie nodded. "I appreciate this," she told him.

He just waved away her words.

Although she worked practically around the clock from then on—preparing as much of the food for the soiree in advance as possible—as with any party, there was always something she had overlooked, something else that needed to be prepared.

In this case, Regina had made a last-minute request for a certain entrée to be prepared because of a special guest who'd agreed to attend at the last minute.

About to check on a few things before they were due to take the food over to Regina's house, Declan saw Josie moving around the kitchen as if she were trying to do two things at once.

It was like watching a lightning-fast Ping-Pong match.

"You forget to make something?" he guessed.

"I didn't forget. There was a last-minute request from Regina—a dish that's a favorite of a special guest," Josie told him. "Now it's up to me to make up over a hundred servings of it."

"You have the recipe?" he asked her, curious.

"That, fortunately, I *do* have. It's for ten servings so I just need to multiply it by twelve so that it yields over a hundred and twenty servings—in less than an hour," she told him.

Declan nodded. "Doable," he told her.

"How? Do you have a magic wand in your pocket?" she asked, setting out baking trays on the kitchen table in a flash of optimism.

"Better than that." He held up his hands. "I have ten fingers. Now, let me see the recipe and let's get moving."

"You're going to help?" she asked him, stunned.

"You're going to stand there and waste time?" he countered, waiting for her to get moving.

Her eyes met his as her smile spread. "Nope, not me," she answered. "Okay, let's get this show on the road," she told him.

Drawn by the sound of their voices, Shannon made her way over to the kitchen table. "Can I help?" she wanted to know.

Right now, Josie would be willing to let Champ help if the dog had had hands instead of paws.

"I can take directions really well," Shannon reminded the woman she idolized. "Just tell me what you want me to do and I'll do it," she promised.

"Good enough for me," Josie replied.

Opening the refrigerator, she pulled out the packages of extra-large shrimp she had purchased at the last minute and set them on the side of the sink. "Let's get started," she declared.

Chapter Sixteen

All the food that had been prepared for the big event was finally packed up and ready to go. Declan was about to begin taking everything out to her vehicle to be transported to Regina Mackenzie's mansion when Josie moved in front of him to stop him.

"Something wrong?" he asked her, confused.

Nothing was actually wrong, except that she felt guilty about imposing on Declan this much. He had already given her access to his kitchen as well as helping her prepare the last minute item.

Josie broached the subject by starting in the middle of it.

"You know, if you have something else to do, I totally understand," Josie told him. "You've already been a great help. Loading up my car is going over and above the call of duty, so to speak. I can take it from here," she said, attempting to let Declan off the hook.

Declan, she noted, didn't look like someone who felt he was being absolved of any responsibilities. Instead, he asked her a question. "This catering thing is a big deal for you, isn't it?"

"Well, if it all goes well, Ms. Mackenzie might ask me to cater another soiree for her. Plus she seemed opened to the idea of throwing a fundraiser for the animal shelter, which is dangerously low on funds right now," Josie told him.

"So it *is* a big deal," Declan confirmed. Moving around her, he picked up the first of the packaged items. "And just so you know, when I tell someone that I'm going to help them, I always keep my word," he told her, heading toward his own vehicle that was parked out front, next to hers. "So stop telling me not to come."

Grabbing one of the packed-up platters, Josie quickly fell into step behind him. She didn't want Declan to misunderstand what she was saying. "I didn't say not to come, I just said you didn't *have* to if you had something else to do."

He turned abruptly to look at her. "Josie," he said sharply.

She braced herself, not at all sure what to expect. "Yes?"

"Stop talking. Because the longer you talk, the colder this food is going to be when it's finally delivered and the less time you'll have to get there and set up. Understand?" he asked point-blank.

Josie nodded, surprised that he had given the whole matter this much thought. "Yes."

"Good, then once we finish loading up the cars, we can go," he said as he resumed bringing out the packaged containers. "Shannon and I will follow you in my vehicle. That way there's more room for the food and it won't run the risk of getting squashed."

That sounded great, Josie thought, starting to go back to the kitchen. Impulsively, she doubled back and, putting her hand on his shoulder, drew Declan over to her and brushed her lips against his cheek.

"Thank you," she said then hurried off to bring out the last of the boxed food to her vehicle.

Shannon looked at her uncle. There was a big grin on her face. "I think she likes you, Uncle D."

Declan waved away the teen's comment. "I think she's just grateful for the help."

Watching Josie come out of his front door, he moved quickly to take the overly large wrapped platter from her. He secured it inside her vehicle. Crossing back to his Jeep, he got in behind the wheel and then started it up.

"Grateful," Shannon echoed. "Right," the teen said, her tone telling Declan that she was not buying his excuse.

"Well, she is," Declan insisted.

"Oh, she's grateful, all right," the girl agreed. "But that still doesn't change the fact that she likes you,"

Shannon concluded in that knowing way that only teenagers were capable of.

Because he didn't want to argue with his niece or, for that matter, let his imagination run away with him on the subject she had raised, Declan decided to turn on the radio.

Shannon made a face at the music that came on, but she decided not to comment on it. For the time being, peace was restored.

Because Josie had called to say they were coming, Elise was waiting for them out in front of her aunt's large house by the time they arrived.

"I'll show you to the back entrance," Regina's niece volunteered. "No offense," she apologized quickly, worried that having them go in the back entrance might make them feel like second-class citizens. "Aunt Regina's guests are going to be parking out here and using the front door," she explained. "We just want to make sure that no accidents happen."

"No offense taken," Josie assured the young woman. Elise struck her as looking even more tense now than she had the first time they had met.

Like participants in a small caravan, Josie and Declan followed Elise's vehicle to the rear of the tall, imposing building. Parking, Josie got out quickly and opened the back of her vehicle, taking out the most accessible items she had packed.

Declan parked his vehicle right next to hers. Frowning, he looked at what Josie was about to carry.

From the aroma he detected, he knew it was part of the main course and the dish was on the heavy side.

He reached for it. Josie moved back, holding the platter just out of his reach. "I can manage carrying it," she assured him.

"I'm sure you can, but I'm not about to play tug-of-war with you over this, so just step back," he told her gruffly, taking hold of the platter Josie was just about to carry in herself.

Listening to the exchange between the caterer and the man she had brought with her, Elise made the logical assumption that the man was there to assist Josie.

"Aunt Regina hired some of her usual waitstaff for this soiree," Elise told them. "I'll go get Mike and Albert," she said before quickly disappearing into the house.

"Looks like she hired some people to help us serve," Josie guessed. "I didn't know," she apologized, seeing the look on Declan's face. "If I did, you could have gone on with your day."

As far as Declan was concerned, he was just where he wanted to be.

"No harm done," he told her. "Never hurts to hone an extra skill, right, Shannon?" he asked, glancing toward his niece.

"Sure," the teenager agreed. She liked being a useful part of this adult world she had been admitted into. "What do you want me to do?" The question had been directed toward Josie.

"For now, you and your uncle can follow the food

inside," she told Shannon. "I am going to remain out here just to make sure they take everything in and don't leave something behind." As she watched, the two men that Elise had referred to as "the waitstaff" started carrying things into the house through the back entrance. "Once they get everything inside, we can get started setting things up."

Josie knew she could leave that to the waitstaff as well, but she preferred doing as much herself as she could, or at least supervise having those things done.

"Wow," Shannon commented. She took in everything that had been set up on the various tables placed along the back wall of the main dining room. "I didn't realize there was so much food."

Her green eyes swept over the entire scene. She was impressed by how much all this had turned out to be. Because she knew she was going to be around food and probably helping to serve it, the teenager had obediently pulled her long red hair back and out of her face.

"The trick is to never leave them hungry," Josie told her. She took one final look around and put the finishing touches on the various arrangements on the serving tables.

Regina had made an appearance several minutes ago, supervising the place settings to make sure everything was up to her standards. Josie held her breath until she saw the woman nod her approval.

"Everything looks just wonderful," she told Josie.

"And smells divine," she added. "My guests will be very pleased."

"We'll stay to serve the food," Josie told the woman. "Unless you'd rather have your staff do that," she added, thinking Regina might prefer the staff she was accustomed to.

"I think, if you don't mind, it would be more fitting if you did that," Regina told her.

Josie wanted all of this to go as smoothly as possible, so she asked, "And between the serving and the cleanup afterward, where would you like to have us wait?"

The question surprised the hostess. "Why, you can wait here in the dining room, with the other guests," Regina answered as if she didn't see how they could have possibly thought anything else. "There'll be music and dancing, and I know for a fact that the food is going to be excellent if you want to have something to eat," the woman said, winking at Josie and her entourage. Leaning forward, she patted Josie's hand. "I'm sure you'll have fun. All the people who attend my parties do," Regina told her then left the room.

"You heard the lady," Josie said, turning to Declan and Shannon. "We have people to feed." Once Shannon turned her attention toward the table closest to her, Josie leaned closer to Declan. "By the way, if you're worried, you don't have to dance."

The small four-piece band that Regina had hired for the occasion was setting up in the far corner of the large room. They were there to provide music to enhance the guests' dining experience. Regina had apparently covered all her bases.

"Why wouldn't I?" Declan asked as he deftly served several slices of brisket to a guest who was the first person to line up right in front of him. Waiting until the man left, Declan turned to Josie and asked, "Don't you dance?"

"I do, but I didn't want you to feel obligated to take me out on the dance floor." Josie then backtracked, realizing that he had said something she had managed to just gloss over. "You dance?" she asked, surprised.

"On occasion." He looked at her. "If the occasion is right," he added.

Soft music gently began to fill the air. Josie could feel herself responding to it. She raised her eyes to his. "And would that occasion be coming up any time soon?" she asked just as she began to serve another one of the guests the dessert she had created for this occasion.

A smile played on his lips ever so slightly. "It might be," he allowed. And then Declan slanted a look in her direction. "Maybe."

She nodded her head. "Nothing like a definite answer," she said, amused.

She wasn't able to read his expression as he said, "Exactly."

By her count, less than an hour later she, Declan and Shannon had served every one of Regina's guests at least once. A third of them more than that.

The food she had prepared, she thought happily, was clearly a hit.

At that point, Elise came by to inform them that her aunt had said they had more than earned a break, which they were being encouraged to take now.

"Aunt Regina said you've done very well," Elise told them. "Her exact words were it was 'time for you all to join the rest of the guests.'"

Josie's eyes swept over the groups of well-dressed people in the room. "I'm not really sure I can pull that off," she murmured under her breath.

Overhearing her, Declan smiled. "Oh, I think you can," he told her. The band began to play another song, one he was more than familiar with. "Would you like to eat or dance first?" he asked her.

Declan noticed his niece moving over to a table that had several young people seated at it. He judged that they looked to be near Shannon's age. Better than that, they also looked to be friendly.

"Okay, I'll call your bluff," Josie told him, making her choice. "Dance."

She was certain that her choice would make Declan back off. Instead, he completely surprised her. Taking her into his arms, Declan began dancing.

Josie was even more surprised that he could move so well.

She made no effort to hide her surprise. "You really *can* dance."

"Did you think I was lying when I told you I could?" he asked.

"Not lying exactly," she admitted then added,

"But the thought that you might have exaggerated did cross my mind."

"I don't lie," he informed her seriously as he turned her around on the floor, "because once you get caught in a lie, people are never certain whether or not what you are telling them is the truth. Once trust is lost, it's lost forever. I don't like living in that shadowy area."

She nodded, believing him. "That's a really good philosophy."

"I don't know how philosophical it might be," he told her, then said truthfully, "it's just the only way that I know."

Relaxing, Josie leaned her head against his shoulder. The music began to take her away. "I'll remember that," she replied.

After spending all those days preparing for the soiree, it felt as if the actual fundraiser was over with much too soon.

As the guests began departing, Josie and company turned their attention to packing up the empty platters, containers and pans.

Regina swept in just as Josie and the others were half finished.

"Everything was just fabulous," the woman told Josie with feeling. "Thank you again for stepping in at the last minute."

Josie smiled at the woman. "My pleasure," she told Regina.

"We never discussed what you were charging,"

Regina recalled, "but I assumed it was the same as my previous caterer." Josie noticed that the woman emphasized the word "previous." Did that mean that Josie was now considered the "regular" caterer? "If your bill came to more," Josie went on to say, "just let me know." With that, Regina handed her a check.

Josie glanced at the check just before she was about to pocket it. Her eyes widened, all but falling out of her head.

Watching her, Regina guessed, "Not enough?"

Still stunned at the amount, Josie told the woman, "Oh, more than enough."

To her surprise, Regina shook her head. "Never admit to something like that," she told Josie. And then the woman smiled. "We'll just call it even. Give me a couple of days to brainstorm and I'll get back to you about holding that fundraiser for the animal rescue shelter," she said.

Then, flashing an even wider smile that took in all three people in front of her, Regina said, "Thank you for your excellent work," just before she went into another part of her enormous house.

"After I take out what the food came to," Josie told Declan and his niece, "I'll split what's left over three ways. Is that acceptable to you?"

Declan turned her down. "There's no need for that. If you recall, we volunteered," he reminded her.

"And my splitting it three ways will be my way of saying thank you for that," Josie countered. She saw the absolutely overjoyed look that was on Shannon's face and could tell how much it meant to the girl, to have her work valued and compensated. That answered it for Josie. "No argument," she told Declan.

"As long as you don't tell me what I have to do with my share," he told her.

"I wouldn't dream of it," she said.

"Fine, then donate my portion to the animal shelter," he told her.

That surprised her. "I'm speechless," she told him.

He smiled at her. "Then I'd say it's money well spent," Declan told her.

When they finally returned to Declan's house, Josie saw that Shannon was all but dead on her feet.

"Go to bed, honey," she urged.

"But there're all these pots and pans to wash," Shannon pointed out, stifling a yawn. "I should help," the girl protested, although not with too much energy or conviction.

But Josie shook her head. "I don't want you falling into the sink and drowning," she told Shannon. "Go to bed," she said more forcefully.

Shannon looked quizzically at her uncle.

He knew what she was asking. "She's the boss, kid," he told his niece. "I'd listen to her if I were you."

"You sure?" Shannon asked, looking back at Josie.

"I'm sure," Josie replied, pointing up to the stairs.

Shannon offered no further argument and went upstairs on rather shaky legs.

When Josie turned from the stairs and walked back into the kitchen, she saw that Declan had his arms immersed in hot, sudsy water and was busy washing a pan.

The sight stopped her in her tracks.

"Declan, what are you doing?" she asked in a hushed voice.

"I thought it would be obvious," he answered. "I'm washing the pots and pans you used to create that feast of yours."

She definitely wasn't accustomed to this sort of help. Her ex never pitched in at all. This was a whole different world to her.

Like a woman in a trance, Josie walked up to Declan and began rinsing off and drying whatever he had washed.

Chapter Seventeen

Josie wiped off her hands. They were finally finished cleaning up the kitchen and putting almost everything away.

It had taken longer than she had expected.

"Well, that's the last of it—unless you're hiding another pot or pan somewhere," she said, placing the last pan on the counter.

Josie decided to leave putting the rest of the cleaned pots and pans away up to Declan. She didn't want to take a chance on messing up his system by putting the items where they didn't belong.

"As far as I know, none of the pots and pans have learned how to walk so, yes, that is the last of them," he confirmed.

Draining the sink, he proceeded to rinse it out and

then dried his hands. "I appreciate you staying and helping with the cleanup," he told her.

It only seemed fair to her. "And I appreciate you letting me use your kitchen and all your pots and pans to prepare those dishes for the soiree," she told him, a smile highlighting her eyes. "I guess that makes us card-carrying members of a mutual admiration society."

Declan didn't comment on that. Instead, he broached another subject. "Would you like to stay a while and have a glass of wine to help you unwind?" he asked. "You put in a really long, hard day. Actually," he amended, "you put in two really long, hard days."

Josie debated the wisdom of accepting his unexpected invitation, then decided that there was nothing wrong with her saying yes. After all, his niece and his mother were upstairs in their rooms. How out of hand could things possibly get?

Smiling at Declan, she said, "A glass of wine sounds lovely."

Leaving the dish towel he had used to dry his hands draped over the side of the sink, Declan led the way into the living room.

"I don't know how lovely you might find the wine, but it's actually a pretty decent label. One of my sister's men friends gave it to her to celebrate her finishing her last stint in rehab." He laughed dryly. "The guy wasn't exactly the brightest bulb in the box. In one of her more lucid moments, Peggy gave the bottle to me so she wouldn't be tempted to relapse." Opening up the cabinet in the living room, he took out an unopened bottle of wine. "Sadly, giving the wine away didn't manage to keep her safe," Declan said.

"How many times has she been to rehab?" Josie asked as she accepted the glass from him.

"Unfortunately, too many times to count." The words weighed heavily. "I used to think that Peggy would clean up her act for Shannon's sake or even for our mother's sake after Dad died. But it turns out that her addiction was stronger," he concluded sadly.

"Well, at least you were there to step up for Shannon," Josie said, focusing on the positive side. "The two of you seem to be getting along really well lately."

He laughed shortly. "Don't make me out to be a saint," Declan warned. "A large part of the reason Shannon and I are managing to get along these days is because of you," he told her. "You're the one who broke through her barriers. I just followed your lead and slipped in through the crack."

She didn't see it that way. "You're being too modest," Josie told him.

"One thing I'm not is modest," Declan said with conviction. "But I do give a person their due and, if any sort of peace has been restored in that girl's life, it's all your doing."

Taking a breath, he set his wineglass down on the coffee table.

Declan was extremely aware of her presence. Working beside her for the better part of the day, that awareness had only managed to grow more and more pronounced. Sitting so close to her now intensified things further.

"You know," he told her, "for a woman who really didn't know her way around a horse when she first came to me, you turned out to be really smart in all the ways that count."

She wasn't sure what he was getting at. Sitting so close to him was scrambling her thoughts, rendering her mind almost useless.

"You kind of lost me," Josie confessed then asked almost shyly, "Was that supposed to be a compliment?"

"It was," Declan confirmed, a smile playing on his generous mouth. "Most people I know already have horse sense."

She nodded, trying to follow what he was telling her. "At least I had enough sense to get riding lessons."

"Which was a step in the right direction," he acknowledged.

She didn't know quite how, but they seemed to be sitting even closer now than they were just moments ago. Had he moved closer, or had she?

Whatever it was, the proximity between them was weakening her resolve to keep her hands to herself.

Josie could feel her heartbeat increasing. She told herself it was just because of the wine. But if she was being totally honest, wine had never affected her quite in this manner.

Declan glanced at her glass and saw that its contents were almost gone. "Would you like a refill?" he asked Josie, beginning to rise to his feet.

Without thinking, she caught hold of his forearm to stop him. He sank back down beside her, waiting for her to explain herself.

"No, that's all right," Josie told him. "One's my limit if I'm going to be driving. Actually, it's more than my limit," she freely admitted.

"It's a really light wine," Declan assured her.

She nearly laughed. "Well, I'm a really light drinker."

He didn't want her to feel as if he were trying to convince her to get intoxicated.

"I wouldn't want you doing anything you didn't want to," Declan told her with total sincerity.

Josie felt another wave of heat washing over her. She struggled to maintain her barriers in place. Still, because she wasn't all that sure, she had to ask, "Are we still talking about the wine?"

His smile was warm and completely unsettling as he looked at her. "I don't know. You tell me, are we?" he asked, turning the question back around to her.

One moment his face was so close to hers, she could almost taste his words.

And then it wasn't close any longer. What it was, was just a breath away from hers.

The very next moment, she could feel the velvety, stimulating impression of his lips brushing against hers. Moreover, she could feel herself surrendering, making her heart pound wildly in response to his kiss.

She knew this was where she should be putting

on the brakes. This was where she stood up, made some sort of excuse or other, and then just walked out the door.

But she didn't.

For some reason she couldn't begin to understand, Josie just couldn't get her legs to work properly. She couldn't get herself to leave, not the sofa or the man. Instead, she moved toward him even closer.

Closer to Declan and to the warm kiss they were sharing.

The kiss deepened even more, causing her head to spin and her very pulse seem as if it were beating out a message in Morse code.

She had never been any good at understanding Morse code.

When Declan drew back, giving them both a chance to catch their breaths, Josie pointed out a very real concern she had.

"How do we explain this if your mother or Shannon comes down and catches us?"

"There is a very simple way we can avoid that happening," he told her. "We could go upstairs to make sure they don't catch us." But, because Declan had always believed in playing fairly, he forced himself to give her a choice. "Unless you'd rather not."

He really hoped that she wouldn't take him up on that.

In Josie's mind, she was already upstairs, in Declan's room, making love with him.

It took her a long second to rouse herself and ask, "What?"

"Unless you'd rather not," Declan repeated. He knew this had to be said, even though he really didn't want to say it. "If you want to go home, then you should go."

And that one sentence was what ultimately managed to win her over. Rather than pressuring her, he was allowing her to make up her mind.

"But I would rather stay," she told him hoarsely, feeling as if she were literally melting.

With her pulse going into double-time, Josie threaded her fingers through his and rose to her feet. She drew him up with her.

From that point on, because she had given her permission, Declan took the lead.

Still holding Josie's hand in his, Declan led them up the stairs to his room.

There were a hundred reasons why she shouldn't be allowing this to happen, Josie thought, following behind him.

And only one reason why she should.

Because she really wanted to.

She hadn't been with a man since before her husband had left her for his nurse. At the time, relations between them had deteriorated and any sort of communication had completely broken down. They'd kept out of one another's way and that, in turn, had greatly contributed to her feelings of undesirability.

Josie saw every single one of the defects of the woman who looked back at her in the mirror every morning.

And with her confidence totally destroyed, her interaction with men became distant and formalized, never passionate or warm.

But despite her resistance to seeing Declan as anything other than her riding instructor, right now she was definitely reacting to Declan on a very tense sexual level.

That had been building up for a while now, she silently admitted.

Josie had never been above the first floor of his house, had never seen anything beyond his kitchen and the living room.

But now everything looked different to her. Different because she wasn't here to pick up Shannon or to prepare dishes for her catering gig. This time, she was here because Declan was here and she wanted to be in his arms and in his bed.

Crossing his bedroom threshold, she could feel her breath catch in her throat.

The sound of his bedroom door closing behind her echoed in Josie's chest. She could feel it reverberate along her arms and down to her very fingertips.

The latter went from icy to hot as, breathing even more heavily, she threaded her fingers through his hair. She could feel him moving closer to her.

Declan didn't hesitate. He pressed his lips against hers, creating all sorts of delicious havoc within her.

Any chance of putting the skids on this feeling— any possibility that she might resist Declan—died a very swift, fiery death.

The very feel of his strong, gentle fingertips moving along her back, delving just under her blouse and touching the bare skin beneath it swiftly burned away the very last of her resistance.

Tomorrow, she told herself, she would probably wind up regretting this move. But tonight tonight she wanted this man desperately, beyond a single shadow of a doubt.

Wanted him now.

Because of this overwhelming passion he was experiencing, Josie felt almost impossibly precious in his arms. Just shortly after he had given her her first riding lesson, Declan could see this happening between them.

He could tell, even before he touched her, how soft her body would feel beneath his hands. Desire drummed throughout every part of him as he ran his hands eagerly against her warm, tempting body.

In very short order, as Declan, in his ardor, kissed her all over, again and again, her clothes began to fall away. They landed in a heap that mingled with his own clothes as he undressed Josie quickly, eager to experience more of her.

Naked, they melted onto the bed, kissing one another over and over again.

Rather than quelling the mounting fire she felt, it only grew steadily more intense. She could literally *feel* it undulate throughout her entire body, growing stronger by each minute.

He wanted to take her this instant, desperately wanted to experience the ultimate release.

But at the same time, Declan wanted what he was feeling to be mutual, not just something that turned out to be one-sided. That meant he had to bring her up to the same threshold of frenzy that was vibrating through him.

So with careful strokes and fervent, hot kisses, he worked to evoke the response from the woman in his arms that he was desperately looking for.

Breathing was growing more and more difficult because her heart was pounding so intensely she thought it would explode out of her chest.

Josie twisted beneath him, trying very hard not to make any of the noises that were so desperately attempting to be released. She did her best to restrain herself. Josie was afraid that she might be overheard by either Ruth or Shannon.

If either one did manage to overhear her, she knew that it would be a complete disaster.

Trying very hard to be silent, Josie channeled what she was feeling through her body, twisting and turning with vigor as she absorbed the wondrous impression his lips made all over her skin.

Her movement grew more and more pronounced in response to what she was experiencing. She loved the feel, the excitement, that contact with his questing mouth created within her.

Breathing more heavily by the moment, Josie kissed him as hard as she could. Then, moving along his body, she branded him with her lips.

She was kissing him over and over again until he felt as if his very body was on fire.

Unable to hold himself back for much longer, Declan moved the woman's nude, tempting body beneath him. Then, with careful, measured kisses, Declan blazed a trail all along her damp torso until he had worked his way down to her very core. Josie's breathing grew heavier and heavier as his tongue flicked over her, creating one heated, soul-stunning climax after another.

Josie pressed her fisted hand against her mouth, desperately doing what she could to keep her cries of fulfillment and joy from emerging.

Her heart hammering wildly, Josie put her hands against his shoulders. She managed to draw him up to her body until her eyes were delving into his.

Josie raised her head up, capturing his mouth.

Declan couldn't hold himself back a single second longer. Moving her legs gently apart with his knee, he entered her. Then, with precise, deliberate movements of his hips, the dance between them began. At first slowly, then with increased fervor.

She could feel the ultimate eruption building within her until, at the last moment, it finally exploded, taking them each to a place they wanted to inhabit exclusively with the other.

She bit her lower lip, determined to keep the cry that rose within her chest from emerging and echoing through the bedroom. But there was no denying how much she wanted to release that cry until it all but surrounded both of them.

Instead, she allowed that sound to be released via her very heavy breathing.

Josie held on to Declan's body tightly for all she was worth.

The eruption vibrated through her, taking her prisoner until finally, an eternity later, it wound up fading away.

She was amazed that once this wonderful, intimate dance was over, Declan didn't just roll over and fall asleep within moments after the lovemaking had taken place, the way her ex-husband always had.

Instead, Declan held her in his arms, hanging on to the sensation they had created until it ceased echoing through his body, leaving a very warm feeling in its wake.

Still holding her, Declan pressed a kiss to her temple. Josie had the impression that this was unusual for him. It wasn't anything that he said to her, it was just a feeling she had.

Feeling incredibly happy, Josie snuggled against him, the feel of his body warming her to the point that she felt extremely content. She drew even closer to him.

"That was certainly a surprise," Declan murmured against her hair.

His warm breath made her shiver in response. "What was?" she asked, wondering if he was focusing on something specific.

"All of it," he told her, pressing another kiss to her forehead.

Feeling sated, Josie had every intention of getting up.

Any minute now.

Instead, she drifted off to sleep within moments.
There was an extremely satisfied smile on her lips
that remained there, even as she slept.

Chapter Eighteen

Josie stirred.

Despite the fact that she had ultimately been up late, her inner alarm still went off. Reluctantly, even before her brain kicked in, she opened her eyes.

It was 4:00 a.m. Dawn would be tiptoeing in soon. She became aware of Declan lying to her right, still very much sound asleep. Josie could feel heat from his body radiating toward her.

All sorts of warm, loving thoughts wove themselves through her mind, but she knew that she couldn't dwell on them.

She needed to leave, Josie thought.

Now.

The fog lifted from her brain. It would be awful if Declan's mother or his niece saw her sneaking out of his room, or even his house, for that matter. Especially if she was wearing the same clothes that she'd had on all day yesterday.

She had to leave now to prevent that from happening.

So, moving very slowly, Josie began to ease her body out of Declan's bed.

She nearly shrieked when she felt his arm unexpectedly close around her waist, holding her fast.

Her heart settled down a little just as she felt Declan nuzzling the side of her neck.

"Where are you going?" he asked softly, his breath warming her.

"Declan, I have to leave," Josie insisted. She thought that why should be very obvious to him.

"Can't you wait a few more minutes?" he asked, deftly moving his tongue along the outline of her ear, sending warm shivers up and down her spine. "The sun's not even up yet."

She could feel her pulse rising again. He was making this really difficult for her.

"We've been lucky so far, but if your mother or Shannon wake up, I have no excuse to give them why I'm sneaking out of here at this hour," Josie pointed out.

His breath continued to heat up her body.

"We could always go with the truth," Declan said as his lips began to move along the side of her neck, all but branding her.

"I'd rather not have to go through that. I don't think you want to do that either," Josie told him.

"All right," he answered reluctantly, releasing his hold. He drew himself up in bed to look at her. "But only if you promise that we can get together again—soon. Maybe Friday?"

"I'd like that," Josie readily admitted. A rosy feeling spread all through her at almost lightning speed. "But right now, I really need to go," she insisted reluctantly.

Released, she began to get out of bed then stopped. She realized that all of her clothes were still on the floor.

And she was nude.

Heat instantly crept up her neck, coloring her cheeks as she pulled the sheet back up to cover herself.

"Turn around," Josie requested, swirling her finger around to point his face toward the wall.

Declan's brow furrowed a little. "Why?"

Was he really going to make her have to explain? Apparently so, she realized with an impatient sigh. "Because I'm not wearing anything."

Declan stared at her. "You're kidding," he said in disbelief. But one look at her face and he saw that she was completely serious. "I've already seen you without your clothes on," he pointed out.

He was definitely going to make her explain this, she thought, resigned. "Yes, but that was in the heat of the moment—and the room was dark. Declan, please. I really need to get dressed and make my getaway," she pleaded.

"All right," he agreed. "Never let it be said that I

gave you a hard time—I mean a difficult time," he amended, an amused smile playing on his lips.

Declan turned his face away from her and toward the wall.

The moment she was sure that he was no longer looking at her, Josie got dressed at what seemed like lightning speed.

In less than three minutes, she had her clothes on and was carrying her shoes in her hand.

Pausing to brush one final kiss on Declan's cheek, she eased his door open and then paused for a moment in the doorway, carefully listening.

She didn't hear anyone stirring either upstairs or down. Taking that as a sign that she was free to make her getaway, she closed Declan's door behind her. Her heart pounding, she flew down the stairs.

Her heart was beating double-time by the time she made it to his front door. Holding her breath, Josie opened the door then quickly closed it behind her as she made her escape.

She all but ran—still barefoot—to where she had left her car parked. After dashing over the gravel driveway, Josie could feel her feet complaining until she was able to get behind the wheel. A sense of huge relief came over her as she rested her feet on the carpet.

Made it, she thought.

The next moment, Josie started up her car. She drove back to her brother's house, heading for her apartment over the garage.

She let out a deep breath as she parked. Sitting

there for a moment, she got out and made her way up the stairs. Reaching the apartment that had been constructed just for her, Josie unlocked the door and went in.

Once inside, she closed the door behind her then dropped her purse on the floor along with her shoes. By everyone's time—except maybe for a rooster's—it was way too early to be awake.

Since Rebekah handled the first feedings, Josie reasoned, that meant that she had about three, maybe four hours at best to take a nap, she estimated.

Lying down fully dressed on the bed, Josie let out a very long, heavy sigh. The odd thing was that she felt both wired and exhausted at the same time.

And exhilarated, she thought as bits and pieces from last night began to replay themselves—in vivid color—through her mind.

It was all so completely wonderful, she couldn't help reliving every single fantastic moment. Declan had been such a thoughtful, gentle lover—and the man washed dishes, too, she mused, her lips curving as she recalled watching him.

Curling up on the bed, Josie replayed the entire evening in her mind. That included everything from working to set up the soiree, to the dances she had shared with Declan—who would have thought that he could have turned out to be such a great dancer?—to the wonderful night they had spent together in his bed.

As she went over the whole thing, from start to finish, it only kept getting better.

And he wanted to do it again, she thought, remembering Declan's last words to her before she had left this morning.

Josie sighed again.

If she had a lick of sense in her head, she would just quit while she was ahead, before the disappointment came, she thought.

But she knew she wouldn't. At least, not yet.

Her thoughts dwelled on Declan again. She had never had an affair before, she realized. For that matter, she had only had one lover before Declan and that had been her ex-husband.

Look how that turned out, Josie's mind taunted her.

The next moment, she rallied. Just because her ex had broken her heart didn't mean that Declan would, she reasoned.

You're forgetting one thing, a voice in her head warned. *Declan needs a younger woman. That isn't you. Get used to the idea that at most, this is just going to be a temporary thing. Wonderful, yes, but still just temporary. Enjoy yourself while you can and then go your own way. This isn't going to amount to "forever."*

It's just some fun, nothing more, she silently warned herself.

Still, Josie thought the next moment, that didn't sound all *that* bad, she reasoned. Last night had been utterly and breathtakingly delightful. Maybe there were a few more of those evenings in her immediate future, she thought. She could live with that.

Except that this time, she told herself, she would make a point of having Declan come to her apartment. She didn't want to risk running into either Ruth or Shannon on mornings after. Anticipating that, even if it wouldn't be foremost in her mind, would definitely put a damper on the evening. It was tantamount to mentally looking over her shoulder the entire time that they made love.

Josie snuggled against her bed. She didn't expect to actually sleep, not with visions of the dances she had shared with Declan replaying themselves through her head.

But without realizing that it was happening, Josie finally drifted off to sleep.

"How did the catering go?" was the first thing Rebekah asked that morning when Josie walked into the main house, offering to help with the twins.

Making her way over to her sister-in-law and the twin in her arms, Josie smiled broadly. "It went really, really well," she said with enthusiasm.

Rebekah had just finished feeding Lily, and was now in the middle of feeding Lucas.

Rebekah's mouth curved. "I heard that you had help," she mentioned a little too casually.

"I did," Josie answered, pausing to wrinkle her nose playfully at Lily. The twin cooed. "Declan and his niece came with me to help with the setup. They also helped me serve."

"Did 'they' help with anything else?" Rebekah asked a little too innocently.

Something in her sister-in-law's voice caught her attention. "What do you mean?"

"That was an awfully big smile on your face just for acknowledging getting some help," Rebekah noted.

"It wasn't just 'some' help. It was a lot of help," Josie emphasized.

Rebekah's smile just grew wider. "Oh, I see." Then, unable to resist, her sister-in-law casually added, "I like Declan."

It wasn't exactly difficult for her to read Rebekah's mind.

"It's not like that," Josie told her, determined to nip any possible misunderstanding in the bud.

Rebekah widened her eyes, giving her the most innocent look she could muster. "Like what?" she quipped. "I didn't say anything, did I, Lukie?" she asked, addressing her remark to her son.

"You didn't have to," Josie told her. "That smile of yours gave you away."

Rebekah cocked her head as she looked up at Josie. "I'm just happy, that's all."

"Uh-huh." Josie tried to salvage the scenario she was attempting to create for Rebekah's sake. "He's a great guy—" she began, only to have Rebekah cut her off.

"I picked up on that from what you've told me," she said with a smile.

Josie stifled a sigh. Maybe she should have this printed up on a card. "But he's also too young for me."

Her sister-in-law frowned, clearly not buying the excuse. "What makes you say that?"

"Rebekah, I'm six years older than he is," Josie pointed out with feeling.

"Oh my. And you're not in a wheelchair yet?" Rebekah pretended to marvel.

Josie didn't appreciate her sister-in-law's remark. "That's not funny, Rebekah."

"No, it's not," Rebekah agreed. She was serious, Josie realized. "It's sad, actually. You're running from the first bit of happiness to come your way in *ages*," the younger woman emphasized. She knew what was behind this and for once she said it. "Not every man is a loser like that ex-husband of yours," Rebekah insisted. "Declan could be the one you've been waiting for."

Josie opened her mouth to protest, but Rebekah held up her free hand, indicating that she should stop talking.

"You need to allow yourself to explore the possibilities, Josie. That means you need to learn to enjoy yourself a little," Rebekah insisted.

Josie sighed, surrendering. "I'll give it a try," she promised.

"You'll do more than that," her sister-in-law told her seriously. "The thing that struck me about you from the very first day that I met you is that you're not a quitter."

"No," Josie allowed, "but on the other hand, I am a realist."

"Since when?" her sister-in-law scoffed with a

laugh. Josie began to protest, but Rebekah wouldn't let her. Instead, she said, "You take on more work than any one person can possibly handle and yet, somehow, you manage to do it all.

"And, if that's not enough, you also got Shannon to come out of her shell in order to help with the animals. Then you jumped in at the last minute to help cater that big fundraiser." Rebekah pretended to wipe her brow. "Whew, I get tired just talking about it," she told Josie with a laugh.

Josie waved away her sister-in-law's words. "You're making me out to be some kind of super-woman," she told Rebekah.

Rebekah didn't look put off. "Well, if the cape fits, wear it" were her sister-in-law's words of wisdom.

Lily began fussing. Her sister-in-law's attention shifted to her immediately.

"Don't worry," Josie said, rocking Lily a little more. "She's all right. You just finish feeding Lucas."

Rebekah smiled at Josie, her point made. "See, like I said, a regular superwoman."

Josie shook her head, giving up. "Okay, have it your way."

"Was he a good dancer?" Rebekah asked a couple of minutes later.

Josie closed her eyes and sighed, remembering.

"He was surprisingly good," she admitted, then added, "Seeing as how the man spends a third of his life astride a horse." And then she looked at her sister-in-law, surprised. "How did you find out that he danced with me?" she wanted to know.

"Josie, this is a small town. The main hobby for most of us is gossip. You dancing with that good-looking cowboy had word spreading like the proverbial wildfire."

Josie frowned. "You're exaggerating," she said dismissively.

"No, I'm envisioning," Rebekah corrected. "Relax, Josie," she assured her. "Nobody's about to call you a scarlet woman."

Her eyes widened. *Rebekah knew*, she thought. "Why would you say that?" Josie cried.

Her sister-in-law suddenly grew silent for a moment. Seeing how pink Josie's face turned, she put two and two together. "You slept with him?" she questioned. "You slept with Declan Hoyt?"

"No," Josie cried. Then, because she hated lying and felt it could only wind up harming her relationship with her sister-in-law, she took back her denial. "Yes," she told Rebekah in a smaller voice.

"Oh, Josie," Rebekah cried. Josie braced herself for a lecture or, at the very least, a show of disappointment. Instead, her sister-in-law moved closer to her on the sofa as she continued feeding her son. "Tell me all about it—or as much as you're comfortable sharing," she amended, not wanting to impose. "Did he seduce you? Did you seduce each other? Was he a great lover, or is that handsome stud a dud?"

"I can't answer all that," Josie protested, growing redder.

"Okay, I understand," Rebekah said, even if she was disappointed at the lack of any significant detail. But then she asked something she felt that Josie could answer. "Are you going to see him again? You know, in *that* way?"

"Well," Josie allowed, "he did say something about seeing me this Friday evening."

Rebekah's face lit up. "Oh, Josie, I am so happy for you!"

"Rebekah, please don't get carried away," Josie warned her.

"I won't," her sister-in-law promised. "That's your job," she said with a wink. Then, looking at the twin in her arms, Rebekah said, "Your aunt Josie's got a date. Can you say 'yea!' Lucas?"

Turning the baby so that he faced Josie, Rebekah pretended to be the twin and declared, "Yea" in a muffled voice.

That made it impossible for Josie to maintain a serious expression and she broke down and started laughing.

Chapter Nineteen

A couple of days went by before Josie was able to swing by in the afternoon to pick Shannon up and take the teen to the animal shelter with her. She hadn't even been able to get together with Declan in that time.

But now she was able to do both.

When it came to Shannon, Josie was very proud of the fact that the teen was managing to get the newest additions so well adapted to their surroundings.

Shannon, Josie thought, had developed into a very remarkable human being. Josie was both proud and honored that she'd had some small part in helping the girl become the thoughtful and caring young woman she was always meant to be.

As for Declan, once things had settled down,

he had come over to her apartment several times. They had spent wonderful evenings together, each one more fantastic than the last. However, in the last couple of days, she had dedicated herself to helping Rebekah with the twins. Lily was teething and Lucas had colic. Both twins were up for two days straight, registering their acute unhappiness loudly. Josie felt it only right to help her sister-in-law since that was the main reason she had come out from Florida in the first place.

When Lily's tooth finally broke through the surface and Lucas's colic had subsided, Josie tried to go back to life as she knew it. Stopping by Declan's house to pick up his niece, she was surprised to find that everyone was home and that there was more than a little tension in the air.

Her first thought was to pitch in and try to help with whatever was going on, because something clearly was.

The shell-shocked expressions on Declan's and Ruth's faces were definitely hard to miss. Out of all three people, it surprised Josie to see that Shannon looked to be the calmest one there.

"Is something wrong?" she wanted to know, looking from Declan to Ruth and then at Shannon. No one said anything at first.

And then Declan spoke up. "You might say that."

Josie usually allowed people to answer her at their own pace, but she could sense that whatever this was, it was just too important to drag out. The sooner she knew, the sooner she could help.

"Well, what is it?" She noticed that Ruth appeared to be completely devastated. The older woman was also avoiding making any eye contact with her.

"Ruth? What's wrong?" she questioned. Declan's mother was still avoiding looking at her. "How can I help?" Josie wanted to know.

Again, it was Declan who answered her. He didn't look very happy about what he had to say.

"It seems that my sister decided to check herself out of rehab earlier than she was supposed to," Declan told her.

Josie knew that checking out early usually wasn't looked upon as a good thing, but there was no law against it. At least, not as far as she knew.

Checking out early usually just raised problems for the family, she thought, glancing at Shannon.

The teenager, she noticed again, appeared totally unfazed by this turn of events. On the other hand, there were unshed tears shining in Ruth's eyes.

"That's too bad, but she can do that, right?" Josie asked, looking to Declan for confirmation.

"Normally, yes," Declan said. "But not when a stint in rehab is being offered in place of a prison sentence. Then it's definitely *not* allowed."

"So now what happens?" Josie asked Declan. "Are you going to try to talk your sister into going back to rehab?" From where she stood, it seemed like the logical thing to do.

"Can't," Declan answered flatly. "It doesn't work that way. Besides," he continued, doing what he could to hold on to his temper, "it's too late for that."

Josie wasn't sure she was following him. "Why is it too late?"

"Because Peggy was arrested shortly after she walked out of the facility," he told her. "Apparently someone there alerted the police and now she's going to prison for the next eighteen months."

When he said that, his mother made a small whimpering sound, like her heart was breaking.

Josie was quick to sit down next to Ruth and put her arm around the woman in an attempt to comfort her.

"It'll be all right," she told Ruth gently. "Maybe this is what Peggy needs to make her realize this isn't just a game. That taking off like that has serious consequences."

Devastated, Ruth began sobbing quietly. "Where did I fail my daughter?" she cried, upbraiding herself.

"You didn't fail her, Ruth," Josie told her. "Peggy failed herself," Josie maintained. Putting her hand on Ruth's shoulder, she raised the woman's head to get her to look at her. "You can't live your children's lives for them, you can just give them the right tools to deal with things and hope for the best," she told the softly sobbing woman.

Still keeping her arm around Ruth's shoulders, Josie looked over at Shannon. "And how are you doing?" she asked sympathetically. This had to affect the girl since it was her mother.

Shannon just raised and lowered her shoulders in an indifferent motion.

"I'm okay." And then the teenager looked toward her uncle. "Looks like I'm going to have to stay here longer than anyone thought, huh?"

"Longer?" Josie asked, still keeping her arm around Declan's mother.

Shannon nodded. "Well, yeah," she asserted. "I was only supposed to be here for the ninety days of the rehab program, but now my mother's sentence is at least eighteen months." She looked at Josie who, she judged, needed to have this clarified. "The sentence could be lengthened for bad behavior and Mom's got a bad temper when she gets mad," Shannon said without emotion. "So maybe she'll have to be there even longer."

"Don't say that, Shannon," Declan said shortly, then collected himself and added in a calmer voice, "Maybe this will put the fear of God into her and she'll finally act like a responsible adult."

Shannon shrugged again. "I wouldn't hold my breath, Uncle D."

"Things still may turn out for the better," Josie told the teenager.

"Josie, could I see you in the kitchen for a moment?" Declan asked.

"Sure," Josie agreed. "Shannon, why don't you take my place over here—" she nodded at the sofa "—and see if you can make your grandmother feel a little better?"

Shannon sat down in the space that Josie vacated and put her arm around her grandmother's thin shoulders. "Everything's going to be all right,

Grandma. At least you'll know where Mom is every night for the next year and a half."

"That's little consolation," Declan murmured under his breath as he led the way into the kitchen.

"Hey, people find comfort where they can," Josie told him.

It was a philosophy she had come to embrace when she had dealt with an overwhelming depression that had all but threatened to swallow her up whole. That was just after her ex-husband had left her.

It occurred to Josie that that was possibly what lay at the root of why she hadn't wanted to get involved with anyone, most especially with Declan. With any man, she would be afraid that if she took her barriers down and allowed herself to fall for him, he would eventually lose interest in her and seek out someone younger than she was. With Declan, the fear was even greater since someone younger might actually be closer to his own age.

All these thoughts were burrowing through her brain as she followed Declan into the kitchen.

But when he turned around to look at her, his was not the expression of a man focusing on the age difference between them. He didn't seem to be focusing on them at all.

He appeared to be miles away.

She didn't have long to wait to find out why he had called her aside.

"I don't know if I can do this, Josie," the breeder confessed.

She wasn't sure just what Declan was referring

to. There was a lot on the table to choose from right now. Was he referring to unscrambling the mess his sister had made of her life, or was it something else?

Instead of asking him outright, Josie attempted to approach the situation diplomatically. "I'm thoroughly convinced that you can do anything, including fly like Peter Pan, if you wanted to, but what are you talking about—specifically?" she emphasized.

Sighing, Declan dragged his hand through his hair, as if that could somehow set this new dilemma straight. "I don't know if I have it in me to be a full-time parent for so long, Josie."

That seemed reasonable enough, she thought. "Nobody knows if they're up to the challenge when they first start out, especially when they're starting out with a kid who's already fourteen years old instead of a newborn. That is pretty scary, but at least you won't have to deal with changing diapers or getting up for feedings every three hours," she noted.

Declan frowned, shaking his head. "That's not funny," he told her.

"I wasn't trying to be funny," Josie clarified. "I was trying to get you to look on the positive side." He really did look worried, she thought. She did what she could to reassure him. "I've spent time with Shannon. Once she shed that tough exterior she had wrapped around herself to keep from being hurt, there was this lovely, caring human being underneath all that," Josie emphasized. "If anything, she's probably more scared about this new situation between the two of you than you are.

"Don't forget," Josie reminded him, "she has been dealing with being abandoned by her mother over and over again for a lot of years now. The best thing you can do is make her feel that her 'Uncle D' is going to make her feel safe," she told him. "Get her grandmother on board, too—once she stops crying," Josie added.

Declan let out a long, loud sigh of relief as he nodded his head. He was well aware that everything that Josie was saying made sense.

Gathering himself together and trying to view the situation as calmly as possible, Declan looked at her. "How come you always seem to know what to say?" he wanted to know.

Josie allowed a smile to curve her mouth. "Years of experience and practice," she quipped. "My daughter might be away at school, but I still text and call Hannah as often as I can. Besides," she added, her smile widening even more, "if I keep talking enough, eventually something I say is going to make sense to you. It's the law of averages," she told Declan. "And I, in case you don't know, am very law abiding."

His eyes washed over her, warming them both. "Among other things," Declan told her.

Framing her face with his hands, Declan brought his face close to hers. He was just about to kiss her when Shannon walked in.

Seeing what she had almost managed to interrupt, the teen looked up at the two people in the kitchen. She innocently asked them, "Did I almost just walk in on something?"

Josie's mind went into overdrive to come up with an acceptable excuse. "Your uncle had just paid me a compliment and was in the middle of giving me a pep talk," Josie explained. "But all that can wait. Did you come in to tell us something?" she asked the girl.

"Yeah. Two things actually," Shannon told them.

"And they are?" Declan prodded, wanting the girl to get to the point.

"Well, first of all, you don't have to worry about me," her words were directed more toward Josie than to her uncle. "I've been through this kind of thing with my mother before. When she used to take off, I'd feel like she was dumping me. I don't feel like that anymore," Shannon said with emphasis. "I know that this doesn't have anything to do with me, it's just my mother's juvenile behavior. She's the one I feel sorry for, but like you said, this might be the best thing to have happened to her. Who knows, she might even wind up growing up," Shannon added philosophically.

"And the second thing you wanted to tell us?" Josie asked encouragingly.

"I think one of you should talk to Grandma and tell her that it's going to be all right. She needs to hear that, and I don't think she's going to believe me if I'm the one telling her."

Josie nodded. The girl was right that her grandmother wouldn't take her reassurances seriously, but she didn't want to be the one to hurt Shannon's feelings by making it seem like her words wouldn't count. So, instead, she found a different way to tell the teen.

She began with a compliment. "That's very sharp of you, picking up on that. As for your grandmother, she feels the way she does because she believes that she's supposed to be the one comforting you, not the other way around."

"But I don't need any comforting," Shannon said, protesting the idea.

"We know that," Josie told her, glancing in Declan's direction. "But maybe, just for now, you should pretend that you do. It might make your grandmother feel better if she thinks she's helping you cope with this situation," she told Shannon. "Rising to the occasion sometimes has the by-product of making that person feel a lot better about everything else that is going on in her life. It's worth a try," Josie urged.

Shannon shrugged. It didn't seem logical to her, but then people weren't always logical. And anyway, she tried not to look indifferent to the suggestion because she liked Josie. "I guess that makes sense— sort of," she conceded.

"Go," Josie encouraged, putting her hands on the teenager's back. "Tell your grandmother how safe she makes you feel, that you know you're going to be okay as long as she's there for you and you can talk to her if the need arises."

Shannon still looked rather dubious. "I'll do it, but I don't know if Grandma's going to believe me."

"With that innocent face?" Josie said, taking the teenager's chin in her hand and turning it one way and then the other as if she was evaluating it. "Of course she will," she assured Shannon wholeheartedly. "Now go back in there. Be your grandmother's sweet angel. Go save the day," Josie added with feeling.

Shannon took the pep talk to heart. She left the kitchen and went back to her grandmother to do as Josie had told her.

Declan made no comment until they were alone again. And then he shook his head as he smiled. "You really are a rather incredible woman, Josie Whitaker. You know that, don't you?"

"I'm just capitalizing on what people already believe in their hearts is true," she told him. "Your mother needs to feel that she can make a difference, that she can help her granddaughter get through this. And believing that is what is going to help her get through the situation," she added.

"You know what'll help *me* get all through this?" he asked Josie.

She began to feel her blood rushing through her veins, but she still managed to ask, "What?" innocently.

"Getting a beautiful woman to spend the evening with me," he told her.

"Well, if I come across one, I'll just pass that on to her," Josie told him with a smile.

Declan laughed, his heart warming as he took her into his arms. "Idiot, *you're* the only beautiful woman I want," he told her.

Then, glancing toward the doorway between the kitchen and the living room to make sure that Shannon wasn't about to come in on them again, Declan quickly stole a life-affirming kiss from Josie.

Leaving the promise of more in his wake.

And soon.

Chapter Twenty

Things just seemed to keep getting better every time she and Declan made love.

If anything, by now Josie would have expected that the aura of magic would have at least begun to wear away, but it hadn't.

Instead, she found that their lovemaking kept climbing to new heights. She also found that Declan definitely wasn't the monosyllabic, gruff man she had met that first day in his stable. Instead, he had revealed himself to be nicer, sweeter and infinitely more caring since then.

That was why, Josie thought with an ache, it was going to hurt so much more when their nights together finally came to an end as she knew that they inevitably would.

But even though she was certain the end was coming, she just couldn't make herself bring it about. Instead, all she could do was just promise herself that she would tell Declan about that inevitable scenario "tomorrow."

"Today" she was going to eke out one more day of heaven to help sustain her when the lonely times finally did arrive.

That was what she was attempting to do, eke out one more day, as she sat beside him in his vehicle. Declan was whisking her off to somewhere secret since he insisted on remaining closemouthed about their destination.

"Declan, where are we going?" Josie asked him again, even more insistently this time.

He gave her the same answer that he had before. "I can't tell you," he said, a smile curving his mouth as he watched the road. "Take it from me. If I tell you, it'll ruin the surprise."

"Isn't that something a kidnapper would say?" Josie asked him.

"I wouldn't know," he answered innocently as he drove his Jeep straight into town. "I don't know any kidnappers."

"Seriously, Declan," Josie insisted. "Where are we going?" she asked yet again.

"I didn't realize that you were so impatient." He chuckled under his breath, getting a kick out of her reaction. "Don't worry, we'll be there soon," Declan promised.

She couldn't shake the uneasiness that had been

slipping over her ever since he had made this suggestion to her and then refused to give her an exact destination.

Making love with him was special enough, Josie thought. She didn't want him going out of his way to do anything else. The more he did, she couldn't help feeling, the more it would hurt once he was gone.

"Can't we just postpone this?" she wanted to know. "I'm probably not even dressed for wherever you're taking me."

Declan spared her a quick, appreciative glance. "You look great," he assured her then added in all seriousness, "Hell, you'd look good just wearing something made out of burlap."

The compliment both flattered her—and worried her. Part of her was afraid that what was happening between them was going much too quickly and that just meant that it was bound to burn out too soon.

And then what?

After it was over, would she still be picking Shannon up to accompany her to the animal shelter? That sort of thing would inevitably entail running into Declan, at least occasionally.

Talk about awkward situations.

"Are you all right?" Declan suddenly asked out of the blue.

Was it possible that he could read the thoughts she was having on her face? She took a deep breath. There was only one way to find out. "What makes you ask that?"

"Well, you stopped talking," he pointed out. "Rather suddenly."

Josie cleared her throat then said the first thing that came to her mind in slow, measured words. "I was just thinking…"

"Think later," Declan advised, pulling up in Veniero's parking lot. "We're here." He gestured at the restaurant right in front of them.

"Here?" she asked, stunned. She looked around like someone waking up from a dream. "You brought me to Veniero's?"

Getting out of his vehicle, Declan circled around to the passenger side and opened Josie's door. "Surprise. Happy early birthday," he told her, helping her out of the Jeep.

"You didn't have to do this," Josie protested with feeling.

"You're using the wrong word," he told her. "I don't *have* to, I *want* to. Let's go in." With that, Declan offered her his elbow.

Josie took it, but she was moving almost in slow motion.

"Don't we have to have reservations?" she asked, thinking he might not have known that. If he hadn't made reservations, then they would be able to just leave and go home.

But Declan's next words dashed that hope. "We have reservations," he informed her with a laugh. "So stop dragging your feet before they wind up giving our table away."

"Wouldn't want that," she told him, resigning herself to the inevitable even though coming here made her feel rather guilty. With all the expenses he had to meet, Josie doubted that Declan could really afford this sort of an indulgence for someone who was just a temporary part of his life.

Josie made one last effort to pull him back. When Declan looked at her quizzically, she said, "Why don't we just go to a drive-thru and order?" she suggested. "After all, what we have to eat really doesn't matter. What really matters is the company."

"Nice try," he told her, "but I insist. This is the most romantic restaurant around, so we'll be eating dinner here. If you want to find a way to thank me, you can do that once we get back to your place. End of story," he concluded. "Now enjoy yourself," he said, trying to keep a straight face. "That's an order."

Declan's words coaxed a smile from her lips. "Well, if I must, I must," she told him.

Declan nodded, feeling somewhat relieved. He had no idea why she was fighting him on this. "That's better," he told her.

When they entered the restaurant, the woman at the reception desk greeted them as if they were old friends. Picking up their menus, she led Declan and Josie to their table.

"I trust this will be satisfactory," she said, then handed each of them their menus.

"This is perfect," Josie replied, taking her seat.

Out of the corner of her eye, she caught the smile on Declan's face. No matter how she felt about this, she knew that Declan had gone to a great deal of trouble to arrange it.

The problem was, she also felt as if she was leading Declan on. It just couldn't continue like this between them. She knew she was going to have to end it—right after one more night with him, she told herself again. If nothing else, she was going to need the memory of tonight to sustain her during the long, lonely nights that would be stretched out in front of her from tomorrow on.

Veniero's more than lived up to its reputation. The restaurant served exquisite Italian cuisine, the kind that literally melted in her mouth and left her palate begging for more.

After some debate, they both ordered the balsamic glazed chicken, with tricolore salad and delicious little chocolate and hazelnut sandwich cookies, which they learned were called baci di bama—lady's kisses. She ate slowly, as if this was to be her last meal.

In a way, it was.

However, all good things, she knew, had to come to an end and so did this. So, once they had finally finished their portions and Declan had paid for their dinners, they found themselves leaving the warm, elegant restaurant.

Holding on to his arm, Josie walked out through the oak-and-glass door. The night air that greeted her was a bit chillier than she had expected. She wrapped both her arms around his one in an effort to generate a little warmth.

Without realizing it, Josie sighed. "I am so full, I'm surprised that I'm not waddling," she confided to Declan as he slowly led the way back to his vehicle.

The image made him laugh. "Well, I happen to think that you'd look cute, waddling, although you're not doing anything even close to that," he thought to add just in case she wound up misunderstanding him. "You know, you're far too critical of yourself," he told her in a moment of seriousness and then said, "Time to take you home, Cinderella."

Reaching his Jeep, Declan unlocked the passenger's-side door for her and held it open. Taking her hand, he helped her get in. Josie buckled up as he closed her door then rounded the hood and proceeded to get in on the driver's side.

He put his key in the ignition. But before he turned it on, genuinely curious, he asked her, "Did you enjoy your dinner?"

"Enjoy it?" she echoed. "Everything was so delicious, I was practically tempted to eat the decorative flowers off my plate," Josie told him sincerely. "That had to be the very best food I'd ever had, bar none. It was just about everything I could do not to ask for the chef's recipes."

"I doubt they would have shared them with you. Restaurants are very possessive when it comes to their recipes. Family secrets and that sort of thing," he told her. For a moment, Josie actually looked disappointed, which had him telling her, "But if we go back enough times, given your background, I think you'd probably be able to recreate at least some of the

meals on their menu. I watched you at that first soiree you catered. You put things together that I would
have never dreamed of combining," he told her.

Declan paused for a moment before finally asking her, "So, what do you say? Where should we go
next Sunday? This place is a little pricey, so it should
probably just be for special occasions, but there are
other options."

Josie had planned to find a way to end their relationship—or whatever this could be referred to that was
between them—by tomorrow. That made next Sunday
seem like it was an eternity away, she thought.

Still, she couldn't find it in her heart to just flatly
turn him down. That seemed too cruel.

"We'll play it by ear," she finally told him eva-
sively.

Declan had no idea why she would word it that
way. Maybe there was something else going on here,
Declan thought. But if he had learned one thing,
it was that women were exceedingly complicated
creatures. That meant that direct questioning almost
never led to direct answers, so for now, he decided to
drop the matter entirely. He didn't want to end this
special evening with anything approximating an argument. What he wanted to do was have the evening
end in her bed, with him holding her in his arms.

When Declan pulled his vehicle up in the space
next to hers, he turned toward Josie and asked, "Is
it all right if I come in for a little while?"

She realized that he never came right out and

asked to do that, not since they had spent their first night together.

Josie searched his face, trying to see if he looked as if he suspected something. But it was way too dark for her to be able to make out his features very well.

So, forcing a smile to her lips, Josie told him, "Absolutely." Moving quickly, she had her door opened and had started to get out of the vehicle. But he turned out to be faster than she was and he had already presented himself on her side.

Offering her his hand, Declan drew her out of the passenger side.

"Watch your step," he warned. "It's awfully dark tonight."

She wrapped her hands around the arm he had extended to her. "Just lead the way."

The stairs on the outside of the garage that led up to her apartment felt almost too steep in the dark. Declan had her walking up in front of him so he could catch her if she lost her footing. He cautioned her to go slowly as he carefully watched each step she took.

He made her feel so protected, she thought. She knew she couldn't allow herself to get used to that, but just for one more evening—before it all blew up on her—she would allow herself to savor the feeling.

Allow herself to pretend that this was never going to end instead of knowing that it would all too soon.

She stopped at the landing right before her door, and unlocked it. Pushing the door open, Josie walked into the apartment first, then glanced over her shoulder to make sure that Declan was following.

Closing the door behind him, Declan began to say something to her, but he never got the chance. Throwing her arms around his neck, she touched her lips to his with a kiss so deep, it wound up taking his very breath away in less than a second.

Her mouth still sealed to his, she continued kissing him as she managed to pull his jacket down his arms. When she had it off, she tossed it aside as she summarily went to work on first removing his tie and then unbuttoning and removing his shirt. She went on kissing him over and over again as she alternated between stripping off the rest of his clothing and pulling her dress off. It fluttered down to the floor as well.

Declan caught her hands just once, holding them together against his chest as he looked at her. His heart was racing.

"Josie?" he asked, hardly able to reconcile this boldly nude woman before him with the one he had come to know these last few weeks, the one who had made him turn away when she had first gotten dressed in the morning. Normally, he'd have liked seeing this confidence in her, and yet tonight, something about her expression made him uneasy.

But she didn't want to talk, didn't want to stop what was happening between them and take it apart, not now. That was for later, when he was no longer with her. This was not the time for words. It was the time to enjoy the very last moment that this would be happening between them.

For his own good, she silently added, because it definitely wasn't for hers.

She could feel tears gathering in the corners of her eyes.

A single drop slithered down her cheek, touching his face. Caught by surprise, Declan pulled his head back and looked at her.

"Josie?" he said quizzically, about to ask what was wrong.

Anticipating his question, she didn't give him the opportunity to speak. Instead, she pushed Declan back onto her bed, a place he had grown so familiar with in such a short amount of time.

Then she proceeded to all but devour him, kissing him all over and branding him with her lips.

It eroded any ability he still had to form a question or even to ask one.

Instead, he found himself quickly rising to the occasion. Declan wound up making wild, passionate love to her, taking her not once but twice, and leaving her almost breathless.

But just as he all but collapsed next to her, Declan could feel her hand lightly gliding over him, taking possession of what had been nearly spent just moments ago. With deft, clever, possessive movements, she had Declan wanting her all over again even though he had been certain that just wasn't in the cards for at least another hour if not longer.

She wound up proving him wrong.

Wound up making him want her with every fiber of his soul. With a last, superhuman effort, he rolled over and proceeded to make love to Josie with slow, deliberate movements, showing her no mercy, taking no respite.

He had no idea why, but he felt there was this urgency, unfounded though it might be, to make love with her one last time before the night faded away into the darkness.

So he made love to her again, putting his very soul into it, determined to wipe out any lingering regrets that she might still be harboring for whatever reason.

Exhausted beyond words, they fell asleep in each other's arms, trying their best to keep the inevitable sadness away that they both felt was hovering just above them.

Chapter Twenty-One

Josie knew she couldn't keep avoiding having this conversation with Declan indefinitely. The longer she waited, the harder it was going to be.

She really hated this feeling that she was leading him on, but that was exactly what she felt she was doing.

Gathering up her courage, Josie took a deep breath and called Declan on his cell. Since she knew that this wasn't the kind of conversation that could be conducted on the phone, when Declan finally picked up, Josie made arrangements to get together later that day. She uttered those words that no one who felt that they were in a relationship ever wanted to hear.

"We need to talk."

There was something in her voice that struck him

as being rather ominous, but he chalked it up as being due to the poor connection.

"Sure, I've got some things to take care of, but I'll be finished by three at the latest. You want to come over then?" he asked, thinking that once they were done, as always, Josie could take Shannon with her to the animal shelter.

Declan had no idea what might be on Josie's mind, but whatever it was, he was confident that it could be easily cleared up.

It did strike him that Josie had seemed preoccupied for the last few days. He was actually looking forward to resolving whatever it was that was bothering her.

"Three o'clock it is," Josie confirmed.

There was a sinking feeling in the pit of her stomach as she hung up.

When three o'clock arrived, Josie felt like a death row inmate who was about to walk their last mile. Driving to Declan's, she must have gone over what she was going to say to him a number of times. Each version was slightly different, but none sounded quite right—not to mention that her sinking stomach now felt like it was tied up in knots.

The sooner she could finally let him down as gently as possible, the better she would feel, Josie thought. In the meantime, her nerves felt as if they were being shredded—not to mention the very real fact that she was already starting to miss him.

When Declan opened the door in response to her

knock, she felt as if she were walking into the house on borrowed legs. Hers hardly felt as if they could support her much longer.

She really needed to get this over with, Josie thought.

One look at her face immediately told Declan that something was very wrong. Whatever was troubling Josie, he wanted to get it out in the open so it could finally be resolved and behind them.

"What's the matter?" he asked her point-blank as he brought her into the living room.

"Declan…" Josie began, feeling like every word she was about to utter was liable to choke her, "we have to break up."

There, she'd said it.

About to sit down, Declan could only stare at her. "Why would you even say something like that?" he wanted to know. "The way I see it, everything has just been getting better and better between us."

Every fiber of her being wanted to agree with him, but she knew that if she did, that wouldn't be fair to Declan. Because Declan deserved someone his own age, deserved to be able to create his own family with a woman young enough to give him children.

She needed to make him understand that this just wasn't going to work between them. If they tried to stay together, then eventually he was going to walk away from her and, when that happened, she wouldn't be able to take it. She was convinced that calling it quits now was better than leaving herself wide open to pain down the line.

Of course, sparing her future self pain meant feeling it *now*.

Searching for an excuse other than the humiliating truth, she thought she'd found one. "Look, you've just taken on a huge responsibility with Shannon, and I applaud you for that," she told him. Pulling her shoulders back, she knew she was going to have to sound heartless, but there was no other way. "But I have already raised my family. I don't want to go through all that again," she told him. "It's not fair to me." Josie could feel her pulse hammering all through her body. "Can you understand that?"

But it wasn't Declan's voice she heard answering her. Instead, Josie heard a heartbreaking sob coming from behind her.

Turning around, she saw that Shannon was standing in the doorway between the kitchen and the living room. She hadn't even heard the teenager come home.

Shannon had walked in just as her idol had vocalized her feelings.

Stricken, Shannon cried, "I thought you were my friend." She pushed past both Josie and her uncle as she raced up the stairs and to her room.

When Declan turned around to face Josie, his expression had changed entirely. There was fury in his eyes, white-hot fury.

"She looked up to you," he accused, "and you just broke her heart. You turned your back on her the same way that her mother always did." This was where he drew the line, Declan thought angrily. "Let me make this perfectly clear. No one, not even you, is ever going to hurt that little girl ever again. Do you understand me?" Declan demanded.

Realizing how Shannon must have felt overhearing her, Josie felt heartsick.

"I didn't realize that she was even there," she said helplessly.

He didn't trust himself to talk to her right now. Struggling to hold on to his temper, Declan told her, "I think you should leave."

There were just no words she could say that would undo the damage she had done. So, listening to his command, Josie left.

Quickly.

He let her go out without another word. As he heard the outer door close, Declan had no idea what to do with the anger he was feeling.

But right now, he wasn't the one who mattered, he thought. The only one who mattered in this scenario at the moment was Shannon.

He had no idea what he was going to say to the girl. He only knew that he had to find some way to get through to her.

Declan hurried up the stairs two at a time.

Just as he had suspected, Shannon's door was closed. At first, he debated leaving her alone to nurse her wounds. But he was well aware that wounds could fester, could very easily get infected. Leaving her alone was the coward's way out.

So he knocked.

"Shannon?" He spoke through the door. "It's Uncle D. Can I come in?"

The only response he heard was the sound of sobs. Ordinarily, Declan didn't believe in intruding, but he knew pain when he heard it and he wasn't about to just leave Shannon like that.

So he announced, "Shannon, I'm coming in."

And with that, he put his hand on the doorknob and turned it. He was surprised when it gave. Shannon hadn't locked the door.

Thinking that was a good sign, Declan let himself in.

He found Shannon on her bed, her face buried in her pillow. But as he entered, the teen scrambled up into a sitting position. She wiped her eyes with the palm of her hand.

Sitting down beside his niece, Declan awkwardly took her into his arms in an attempt to try to comfort her. It was at that moment that he realized they really needed one another. He needed Shannon every bit as much as she needed him.

"I'm not going to ask if you're okay," he told her. "Only an idiot would think that you were all right after that. But I just want you to know one thing, and I want to make it perfectly clear." He raised her head so that she could look at him. "You will always, *always* have a home here with me for as long as you want."

Wiping away more tears, Shannon sniffled. Her eyes met her uncle's. "Really?" she asked, almost afraid to believe him.

Declan put his arms around the teenager again and pressed a kiss to her forehead. "Really," he assured her in a warm, friendly voice.

His niece leaned into him, resting her head on his shoulder. She was obviously comforted by his words.

They remained that way for several minutes.

Declan couldn't get what Josie had said out of his mind. Once he calmed down and got over the chaos her words had created, he began to reexamine the whole incident right from the very beginning. That was when he realized the sentiments Josie had expressed the day before were completely out of character for her.

Since the very beginning, she had been the one to urge him to try to communicate with his niece, to listen to her and reach out to her to strengthen their connection. She was the one who had volunteered to take the teen to the animal shelter with her so that the girl could get involved with both training and caring for the animals.

Yes, Josie got free horseback riding lessons for herself in exchange for working with his niece, but it was abundantly apparent to the man that she gave much more than she got in this exchange. *That* was the Josie he knew—the one who valued family and would do anything to be there for the ones she loved.

For proof, he had the fact that Josie had uprooted her whole life so that she could help look after her niece and nephew. That was not a woman who shunned taking on extra child-rearing responsibilities, who would walk away from a relationship just because it suddenly involved raising a teenager. A teenager who, he knew for a fact, Josie actually happened to like a great deal.

So then, why had she suddenly declared that his custody situation meant they had to break up? The question nagged at him.

The fact of the matter was that Declan knew Josie could easily take on the responsibility of raising another teen—and so did she, he thought.

So just what was behind this sudden about-face he had witnessed?

Was he somehow at the root of all this? Was Josie afraid of relationships because her husband had walked out on her?

He thought back to the time they had spent together. They'd gotten along really well, and that had been mostly her doing, he recalled. But there was that one sticking point she had raised very early in their relationship.

For some reason, the age difference between them bothered her.

Declan hadn't brought it up afterward because he had a feeling that the more he pushed, the more she would resist. Now he wondered if that was truly the reason why she'd ended things between them.

And if it was, what then? If she struggled with feelings of inadequacy, he couldn't fix that for her. She needed to come to terms with that on her own, he decided.

For now, he would just let the matter go. What he

really needed to focus on right now was attempting to mend the rift that had almost taken down his relationship with his niece.

Declan began thinking about what he could do to fix it.

Maybe, he decided, he could open negotiations by offering Shannon a gift.

But what?

And then he remembered how taken the teen had been with Champ when she had first met the dog—and how hurt she had been when the Australian shepherd completely ignored her despite all of her attempts to win him over.

A pet, Declan decided. He could get Shannon a pet of her very own. Thinking, he tried to remember which ones she had talked about when she would come home from helping out at the shelter. He remembered that she had been involved in socializing a number of the newest additions. The problem was, try as he might, Declan couldn't remember any of their names.

The simplest, most direct approach, he knew, would be to take Shannon to the shelter with him after school. Then she would be able to select one of the dogs she had put so much work into training. Her favorite one, he thought. But the problem with that approach would be that she might not be able to pick just one. And besides, taking her with him would spoil the surprise, and he definitely wanted to surprise her. After what she had been through, he felt she deserved something nice happening to her, he thought.

Well, someone at the shelter had to keep track of the dogs and puppies Shannon had worked with, Declan reasoned. Or at the very least, there might be some sort of a record kept in the main office.

Declan recalled having met the director of the animal shelter before. He had been out with Josie when they'd run into her. If he went to her alone, she might start asking him questions about why Josie hadn't come with him, which could turn out to be extremely awkward.

But he couldn't concern himself about that right now, Declan thought. He needed to tackle one problem at a time, he told himself. First, he wanted to comfort Shannon and bridge any gap that might have been created by yesterday's incident.

Once he'd managed to take care of that, then he could get himself involved in other things, Declan thought—and he was certainly looking forward to that. He intended to make Josie see that he was nothing like her ex-husband. The fact of the matter was, he had never cheated on anyone in his life. Even in his casual relationships—and looking back on them now, pretty much all of them prior to Josie had been casual.

He'd gone out with his fair share of women over the years—but he had never been in love with any of them before. Certainly not to the point that he had entertained the idea of sharing a life with one of them.

Declan had actually begun to feel that that sort of attraction just wasn't in the cards for him.

And then Josie had come into his life.

He had never met anyone quite like her before and now that he had, he wasn't going to allow her to just walk out of his life like that.

Certainly not without giving him a damn good reason why—because that excuse she'd given him was nonsense from start to finish, and they both knew it.

First things first, though, Declan quietly told himself.

He wanted to find Shannon a pet of her very own. One she felt was strictly and exclusively hers. That was what his niece needed so that she could feel like she was a part of something.

Baby steps, he thought.

Declan smiled to himself, remembering the first time he had laid eyes on Champ. The dog had just showed up one day. He'd been a puppy at the time—cold, wet, and shaking in a far corner of the stable. When Declan had first spotted the puppy and approached it, Champ had tried to disappear beneath a layer of hay that was in the stall. The poor thing hadn't even growled, Declan recalled, just whimpered.

After several attempts, he had finally managed to coax the puppy out, using a bit of chicken to tempt him. But even using that, it had taken some doing to fully win the animal's trust. When the stray had finally crawled out, taking the food that was being offered, it struck Declan how small, frightened and pathetic the puppy really was.

"Don't you worry," he had said to the dog whose attention had been totally focused on the food. "You're a frightened little dog now, but someday, you're going to be a real champ."

The moment the words were out of his mouth, Declan had stopped and considered the word he had used. "That's what I'll call you," he decided. "Champ. You like that, Champ?" he'd asked in a more assertive tone.

The stray had paused to look up at him, cocking his head as if to absorb the word better. It had made Declan smile. "Okay, Champ it is."

The dog had remained devoted to him from that day forward.

Declan just hoped it would be that easy to find the right dog for Shannon today.

Chapter Twenty-Two

When Declan finally found a volunteer at the pet shelter to ask about the director's whereabouts, he was told that Bethany had gone to a midmorning meeting. Unfortunately, the meeting was taking place off-site.

Left on his own, Declan made his way around the immediate area. He was looking for someone else who could help him find records that might give him a clue about which of the strays Shannon had taken a particular liking to.

Apparently, today wasn't a day that many of the volunteers had decided to come in. The two volunteers he had come across so far looked as if they more than had their hands full. They certainly didn't have any time to answer his questions.

Undaunted, he went in search of another, hopefully more helpful, volunteer.

Spotting a woman with her back to the doorway, Declan hurried over to catch her before she became involved in another task. It was only as he drew closer that Declan recognized who he was approaching.

Josie.

Unprepared for any sort of confrontation with her, he was about to turn around and leave the area when he realized that Josie's shoulders were trembling the way they would if she were crying and attempting to stifle any telltale sound.

He couldn't just walk away now.

She seemed totally oblivious to her surroundings.

Stepping around Josie to face her, he said her name. "Josie? Are you crying?"

Startled, she looked up, simultaneously wiping the tear streaks from her face.

"No," she denied with feeling, her voice cracking.

Declan ran a thumb along her damp cheeks. "Then what's this?" he asked, holding up his thumb for Josie to look at.

"Tears," she finally admitted.

Josie raised her eyes up to his face. She knew she might as well come clean. "I can't tell you how terribly upset I feel about Shannon overhearing what I said to you yesterday." She wiped off the rest of her tears, slipping the tissue into her pocket. "What are you doing here?"

"I thought that after everything Shannon has gone

through lately, maybe getting her a pet of her own might be a good idea. It would give her something to take care of, and make her feel like the ranch is really her home," Declan explained.

Josie nodded. He was a really good guy, she couldn't help thinking.

"That's a very good idea," she told him. Taking another breath to pull herself together, Josie told Declan, "And I have just the dog for her. Wait right here," she said, turning to head to another part of the shelter.

But Declan didn't want to let her out of his sight. He was afraid she might bolt again. "If you don't mind, I'll just go with you."

A sad smile curved her lips. "Don't trust me?" she guessed.

"I just don't want to take a chance on getting lost," he joked. "This is rather a large facility."

Josie laughed softly. "You know, for a second, I almost believed you."

"I'll work on it," Declan told her matter-of-factly.

"This way, please," she said, leading the way to one of the rooms. "I have just the dog for Shannon," she repeated. Walking into the room where there were several dogs, Josie brought Declan over to an amiable-looking puppy with curly black-and-white fur. "Meet Harlow," she said.

Declan looked dubiously at the dog. "What is that?" he wanted to know.

Josie picked the dog up. "Harlow is a cockapoo," she explained. "That's half cocker spaniel, half poodle. And before Shannon came into her life, she was this pathetic, terrified dog that wouldn't respond to anyone. Several of the volunteers had written her off as being too shy to be trained. But your niece changed all that," she told Declan proudly. "You know, she has a real knack for training hard-to-work-with dogs. You should be very proud of her," she added.

"I am." Declan took the dog from her, holding him against his chest. "Looks like you've just found yourself a home, Harlow." Still holding the puppy, Declan looked at Josie. "Why don't you show me what papers I need to sign and where to pay for this little pup," he requested.

Josie really wanted to get away, but she just couldn't leave this adoption up in the air. It needed to be completed.

"Sure," she said, "I'll take you."

Declan waited until everything involving Shannon's new pet had been taken care of. Afterward, Josie felt their business was concluded.

"Well, I guess I'll see you around," she told him, then added, "If you get a chance, let me know how Shannon liked her surprise gift."

But as she handed him the leash, Declan slipped it on to his wrist and made up his mind. It was now or never.

Determined to stand his ground, he caught her hand in his to keep Josie from escaping.

When she tried to pull free, he didn't release her.

"Josie, why can't you see a future for us?" he wanted to know.

Oh please not that, she thought. "You know why," she said out loud.

"The age difference again?" he asked in disbelief. "You know that doesn't matter to me. When you're ninety, I'll be a spry eighty-four and I'll probably still be chasing around after you," he told her.

She laughed despite herself, shaking her head. "Don't make me laugh, Declan."

"Don't make me cry, Josie," he countered. "Now tell me the *real* reason you're balking at the two of us being together."

"All right," she cried. "If you insist on knowing why I won't be with you, it's because I'm afraid."

"Afraid?" he questioned, confused. That didn't make any sense to him.

"Yes, afraid," she confirmed. "Afraid of giving away my heart again. When my ex left me, my self-esteem completely plummeted. We were together for so long. He was my first…everything. But then he got tired of me and moved on to a newer model. I couldn't bear the thought of that happening again— of loving someone and seeing his love for me fade. It's just a matter of time before you grow tired of me just the way he did."

Declan caught her hands in his again, keeping her from leaving. "Can't you get it through that thick head of yours? I love you, Josie. Moreover, I'm *in* love with you. That's something I've never told another woman before you. I love you and I want to spend the rest of my life with you.

"I can't imagine living even another five minutes without you," he stressed. "Now, what do I have to do to convince you? To get you to believe me? Because I don't intend to let up until you do," he informed her. "Do you want it written in blood?" he offered.

"No, no, this'll do," she told him, finally beginning to smile.

"So you'll marry me?" he asked.

She stared at him, flabbergasted. She hadn't realized that he was proposing. "You're serious?" she cried.

"Are we going to have to go through all this again?" he asked her. "And now you're crying again," he realized. "Why are you crying?" he wanted to know.

"Lots of women cry when someone they love asks them to marry them," she told him.

He took out a handkerchief and wiped her tears, smiling. So she loved him too, he thought, relieved. "Then it's yes?"

She nodded her head, for a moment not trusting her voice. And then she finally said, "Of course it's yes."

"Good, then let's go home and tell Shannon the good news." He felt a tug on the leash. He had almost forgotten that he was still holding on to Harlow. "Oh, and to bring Shannon her puppy," he added, grinning.

"Absolutely," Josie happily agreed.

"Right after I kiss you again," Declan told her. "I've gotten out of practice since the last time."

And then, Declan sealed his lips to hers just to assure himself that he hadn't gotten *that* much out of practice.

He hadn't.

Epilogue

"Mom!" There was no mistaking the pleasure in her daughter's voice as she answered her cell phone. Using the FaceTime feature, Hannah pretended to glare at her mother. "I was beginning to think that you lost my phone number!"

"Said the daughter who hasn't called me in almost a week," Josie countered, amused.

"I have a paper due, Mom," Hannah protested by way of an explanation.

"Let me guess. You used up all your words on the paper, so there were none left over for me," Josie deduced.

"I did have to use some of that time to get some sleep," Hannah said. "You don't want me falling asleep in class, now, do you?"

"Heaven forbid," Josie said, glancing at Declan and smiling. She was really looking forward to introducing her daughter to him. "The important part is that we've finally connected."

"And you have something to tell me," Hannah concluded.

Her daughter had managed to surprise her. "How did you—"

"Mom, please. Even without FaceTime, I can see right through you. Speaking of which, you need to focus the video a little better."

Josie didn't need any further prompting. "I'm doing it right now, my love."

The next moment, Josie managed to clear up the picture of the camera on her cell phone.

She also managed to arouse her daughter's curiosity.

"Mom, who are all those other people in the room with you?" she asked.

Josie had Declan, Shannon and Declan's mother, Ruth, standing beside her. Ruth and Shannon both waved at the girl. "Hannah," Josie began, "I would like to introduce you to—"

She didn't get a chance to finish. Hannah squealed, obviously excited. "Is that… Declan? He's that good-looking cowboy who gave you those riding lessons, right?" her daughter asked, clearly pleased. And then she gasped as her eyes caught a flash on her mother's hand as she took hold of Declan's, pulling him closer.

"Is that a ring on your finger?" Hannah wanted

to know. Not waiting for an answer, she cried, "It is, isn't it?"

Josie turned toward Declan. "Nothing gets by my daughter. She's going to make a fantastic doctor," she told him proudly.

This was clearly after the fact, but Declan decided to properly introduce himself. "Hello, Hannah. I'm Declan Hoyt. And this is my niece, Shannon, and my mother, Ruth," he told the broadly smiling young woman.

She nodded at both women, then said, "Hello, Declan. Are you calling to tell me that you're going to make an honest woman of my mother?"

The greeting stunned him. "How did you—" he began, amazed.

Hannah laughed, pleased with herself. "Mom talked about you enough for me to make the connection."

Embarrassed, Josie started to protest. "Hannah, I never—"

"You didn't have to," Hannah replied, her eyes sparkling even over FaceTime. "Some things I can figure out for myself. So, when's the big day?" she wanted to know, delighted as she looked from one to the other parties involved.

"We haven't figured it out yet," Declan admitted. "Maybe you can help us decide when you come out for your next visit."

Hannah looked extremely pleased as she returned Declan's gaze. "I like him already, Mom. I'll be out the next break that comes up," she promised. Her voice filled with excitement. "I've got lots of ideas."

Declan laughed. "Sounds like a chip off the old block," he told Josie.

"Hey, watch that 'old' stuff," Josie warned.

He smiled at his fiancée, his eyes completely focused on her. "Oh, I fully intend to," he promised. "I fully intend to."

* * * * *

Look for the next book in the
Furever Yours continuity,
The Bookshop Rescue
by Rochelle Alers,
on sale May 2022
wherever Harlequin Special Edition
books are sold.

And catch up with the previous book in the
Furever Yours series:
Home is Where the Hound Is
by Melissa Senate
On sale now!

#2905 SUMMONING UP LOVE
Heart & Soul • by Synithia Williams

Vanessa Steele's retreated to her grandmother's beach house after she loses her job and her fiancé. When she finds out her grandmother has enlisted hunky Dion Livingston and his brothers to investigate suspicious paranormal activity, the intrepid reporter's skeptical of their motives. But her own investigation discovers that Dion's the real deal. And any supernatural energy? Pales compared to the electricity that erupts when the two of them are together...

#2906 A FORTUNE IN THE FAMILY
The Fortunes of Texas: The Wedding Gift • by Kathy Douglass

Contractor Josh Fortune is happy to be Kirby Harris's Mr. Fixit. Repairing the roof of Kirby's Perks is a cinch, but healing her heart is a trickier process. For three years the beautiful widow has been doing everything on her own, and she's afraid to let down her guard. She thinks Josh is too young, too carefree—and way too tempting for a mama who has to put her kids first...

#2907 SECOND-CHANCE SUMMER
Gallant Lake Stories • by Jo McNally

For golf pro Quinn Walker, Gallant Lake Resort's cheery yet determined manager, Julie Brown, is a thorn in his side. But the widowed single dad begrudgingly agrees to teach his sassy coworker the game he loves. As their lessons progress, Julie disarms Quinn in ways he can't explain...or ignore. A second chance at love is as rare as a hole in one. Can these rivals at work tee it up for love?

#2908 THE BOOKSHOP RESCUE
Furever Yours • by Rochelle Alers

Lucy Tucker never imagined how dramatically life would change once she started fostering Buttercup, a pregnant golden retriever. The biggest change? Growing a lot closer to Calum Ramsey. One romantic night later, and they're expecting a baby of their own! Stunned at first, steadfastly single Calum is now dutifully offering marriage. But Lucy wants the true-blue happy ending they both deserve.

#2909 A RANCH TO COME HOME TO
Forever, Texas • by Marie Ferrarella

Alan White Eagle hasn't returned to Forever since he left for college eight years ago. But when a drought threatens the town's existence, the irrigation engineer vows to help. An unlikely ally appears in the form of his childhood nemesis, Raegan. In fact, their attraction is challenging Alan's anti-romance workaholic facade. Will Alan's plan to save Forever's future end with a future with Raegan?

#2910 RELUCTANT ROOMMATES
Sierra's Web • by Tara Taylor Quinn

Living with a total stranger for twelve months is the only way Weston Thomas can claim possession of his Georgia family mansion. If not, the place goes to the dogs— seven rescue pups being looked after by Paige Martinson, his co-owner. But when chemistry deepens into more powerful emotions, is the accountant willing to bank on a future that was never in his long-term plans?

"You still don't belong here." Mariella crossed her arms over her chest, and Alex commanded himself not to notice her body, perfect as it was.

"That makes two of us, and yet here we are."

"I was here first," she muttered. He'd heard the argument before, but it didn't sway him.

"You're not running me off, Mariella. I needed a fresh start, and this is the place I've picked for my home."

"My plan was to leave the past behind me. You are a physical reminder of so many mistakes I've made."

"I can't say that upsets me too much," he lied. It didn't make sense, but he hated that he made her so uncomfortable. Hated even more that sometimes he'd purposely drive by her shop to get a glimpse of her through the picture window. Talk about a glutton for punishment.

She let out a low growl. "You are an infuriating man. Stubborn and callous. I don't even know if you have a heart."

"Funny." He kept his voice steady even as memories flooded him, making his head pound. "That's the rationale Amber gave me for why she cheated with your fiancé. My lack of emotions pushed her into his arms. What was his excuse?"

She looked out at the street for nearly a minute, and Alex wondered if she was even going to answer. He followed her gaze to the park across the street, situated in the center of the town. There were kids at the playground and several families walking dogs on the path that circled the perimeter. Magnolia was the perfect place to raise a family.

If a person had the heart to be that kind of a man—the type who married the woman he loved and set out to be a good husband and father. Alex wasn't cut out for a family, but he liked it in the small coastal town just the same.

"I was too committed to my job," she said suddenly and so quietly he almost missed it.

"Ironic since it was your job that introduced him to Amber."

"Yeah." She made a face. "This is what I'm talking about, Alex. A past I don't want to revisit."

"Then stay away from me, Mariella," he advised. "Because I'm not going anywhere."

"Then maybe I will," she said and walked away.

Don't miss
Wedding Season *by Michelle Major,*
available May 2022 wherever
HQN books and ebooks are sold.

HQNBooks.com ·

PHMMEXP0322

Get 4 FREE REWARDS!

We'll send you 2 FREE Books plus 2 FREE Mystery Gifts.

FREE Value Over **$20**

Both the **Harlequin® Special Edition** and **Harlequin® Heartwarming™** series feature compelling novels filled with stories of love and strength where the bonds of friendship, family and community unite.

YES! Please send me 2 FREE novels from the Harlequin Special Edition or Harlequin Heartwarming series and my 2 FREE gifts (gifts are worth about $10 retail). After receiving them, if I don't wish to receive any more books, I can return the shipping statement marked "cancel." If I don't cancel, I will receive 6 brand-new Harlequin Special Edition books every month and be billed just $4.99 each in the U.S or $5.74 each in Canada, a savings of at least 17% off the cover price or 4 brand-new Harlequin Heartwarming Larger-Print books every month and be billed just $5.74 each in the U.S. or $6.24 each in Canada, a savings of at least 21% off the cover price. It's quite a bargain! Shipping and handling is just 50¢ per book in the U.S. and $1.25 per book in Canada.* I understand that accepting the 2 free books and gifts places me under no obligation to buy anything. I can always return a shipment and cancel at any time. The free books and gifts are mine to keep no matter what I decide.

Choose one: ☐ **Harlequin Special Edition** ☐ **Harlequin Heartwarming**
(235/335 HDN GNMP)   **Larger-Print**
(161/361 HDN GNPZ)

Name (please print)

Address   Apt. #

City   State/Province   Zip/Postal Code

Email: Please check this box ☐ if you would like to receive newsletters and promotional emails from Harlequin Enterprises ULC and its affiliates. You can unsubscribe anytime.

Mail to the Harlequin Reader Service:
IN U.S.A.: P.O. Box 1341, Buffalo, NY 14240-8531
IN CANADA: P.O. Box 603, Fort Erie, Ontario L2A 5X3

Want to try 2 free books from another series! Call 1-800-873-8635 or visit www.ReaderService.com.

*Terms and prices subject to change without notice. Prices do not include sales taxes, which will be charged (if applicable) based on your state or country of residence. Canadian residents will be charged applicable taxes. Offer not valid in Quebec. This offer is limited to one order per household. Books received may not be as shown. Not valid for current subscribers to the Harlequin Special Edition or Harlequin Heartwarming series. All orders subject to approval. Credit or debit balances in a customer's account(s) may be offset by any other outstanding balance owed by or to the customer. Please allow 4 to 6 weeks for delivery. Offer available while quantities last.

Your Privacy—Your information is being collected by Harlequin Enterprises ULC, operating as Harlequin Reader Service. For a complete summary of the information we collect, how we use this information and to whom it is disclosed, please visit our privacy notice located at corporate.harlequin.com/privacy-notice. From time to time we may also exchange your personal information with reputable third parties. If you wish to opt out of this sharing of your personal information, please visit readerservice.com/consumerschoice or call 1-800-873-8635. **Notice to California Residents**—Under California law, you have specific rights to control and access your data. For more information on these rights and how to exercise them, visit corporate.harlequin.com/california-privacy.

HSEHW22

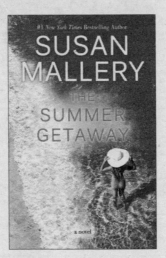

SPECIAL EXCERPT FROM

H **HARLEQUIN**
SPECIAL EDITION

*For golf pro Quinn Walker, Gallant Lake Resort's cheery
yet determined manager, Julie Brown, is a thorn in his
side. But the widowed single dad begrudgingly agrees
to teach his sassy coworker the game he loves. As their
lessons progress, Julie disarms Quinn in ways he can't
explain...or ignore. A second chance at love is as rare as
a hole in one. Can these rivals at work tee it up for love?*

Read on for a sneak peek at
Second-Chance Summer
*the next book in the Gallant Lake Stories miniseries
by Jo McNally!*

"Look." Quinn's eyes narrowed dangerously. "If this
game is that simple, why are you here? If anyone here
should feel like they're being punked, it's *me*. You
obviously expect to become magically competent at
a game you have no respect for without putting in any
of the work. I don't know what motivated you to take
lessons, but if you're not going to work at it, don't waste
my time."

Her whole body went still. Even her lungs seemed
to pause. She'd never been good at hearing criticism,
especially from men. And Quinn had just used a whole
bunch of trigger words. She could hear her mother's voice
in her head. *You never listen. You're lazy. Stupid. You
want motivation? I'll give you some damn motivation—
come here...*

"Julie? Hey, I'm sorry..." Quinn's voice was softer now, edged with regret. She couldn't look at him. She was usually able to control her reactions, but right now she didn't trust herself not to break and either burst into tears or rip into him in a screaming tirade. It had been a long time since she'd done either, but Quinn managed to break through her usual defenses. That realization shook her.

"I've gotta go." She pushed past him, swatting at his hand when he tried to grip her arm. "Don't do that. Just... I need to go. Sorry." She mumbled the last word and kicked herself for it. Apologizing to scolding adults had been her fallback position since she was five. *Sorry, Daddy. Sorry, Mommy. Please don't be mad. Please don't...*

She broke into a near jog toward her car, ignoring Quinn's voice calling after her. He watched in obvious confusion as she drove off. To his credit, he didn't try to stop her. She held herself together until she was off resort property and on the main road, then she cried all the way home. Groceries would have to wait until she could stuff all the ugliness back into the mental vault and pull herself together.

And then she'd have to figure out a way to never, *ever* face Quinn Walker again.

Don't miss
Second-Chance Summer *by Jo McNally,*
available May 2022 wherever
Harlequin Special Edition books and ebooks are sold.

Harlequin.com